CW00433927

WEBS OF BLOOD AND SHADOWS
by
David Dowson

www.daviddowson.com
www.daviddowson.co.uk
daraarts@sky.com

Acknowledgements
Special thanks to my mother, Beryl, who is always there for me and my sister, Jan Webber, author of the Betty Illustrated Children's books.

Edition one
Copyright © David Dowson 2023

www.daviddowson.com
www.daviddowson.co.uk
daraarts@sky.co.uk

Other books also written by David Dowson include:

Chess for Beginners
Chess for Beginners Edition 2
Into the Realm of Chess Calculation
Nursery Rhymes
The Path of a Chess Amateur
CHESS: the BEGINNERS GUIDE eBook:

NOVELS

Declon Five.
Dangers within
The Murder of Inspector Hine
Spooks Scarlett's Enigma
The Deception Unveiled
Webs of Blood and Shadows

TABLE OF CONTENTS

WEBS OF BLOOD AND SHADOWS.............0

CHAPTER ONE 5

CHAPTER TWO...17

CHAPTER THREE..53

CHAPTER FOUR...98

CHAPTER FIVE 162

CHAPTER SIX 215

CHAPTER SEVEN...240

CHAPTER EIGHT 302

CHAPTER NINE 324

CHAPTER TEN...363

CHAPTER ONE

Sebastian Briggs and Christopher Shaw found themselves amid a challenging investigation. Alexander Q, also known as Q, their superior or the one who assigned them the task, had given them a list of businesses to investigate, and despite their exhaustion, they had no choice but to continue their work.

As they descended the worn-out stairway, Sebastian deliberately slowed, aware of his tired feet and the protesting muscles in his calves and thighs. Christopher followed behind, his footsteps echoing the weariness of their task.

The time on Sebastian's watch read four-thirty, indicating that they had been at it for quite some time. The dreary nature of their work only added to their fatigue, but the responsibility assigned by Q compelled them to persist.

The list of businesses they were investigating held some significance, whether it be potential connections to an ongoing case or a broader investigation into an organised crime network. Sebastian and Christopher understood the importance of their mission, which drove them to continue despite their physical weariness.

As they reached the bottom of the stairs, they took a moment to catch their breath and gather their thoughts. They knew that they had to push through and complete the investigation to the best of their abilities. Resigned to their fate, they set off again, determined to uncover the truth behind the businesses on their list and bring any wrongdoers to justice.

The two men reached the bottom of the staircase, entering a dimly lit hallway lined with closed doors and flickering fluorescent lights. The air was musty, carrying the scent of neglect and decades of accumulated dust. The building they were in had seen better days, its dilapidated state reflecting the lack of care it had received over the years.

Christopher, a young and eager recruit, appeared determined despite the weariness etched on his face. Sebastian paused, glancing over his shoulder to ensure Christopher was keeping up. Sebastian knew the feeling well, having experienced countless hours of thankless legwork during his early days in the field.

They had been assigned to investigate a series of seemingly unrelated businesses; their mission was veiled in secrecy. The purpose of their inquiries remained undisclosed, leaving Sebastian and Christopher to navigate through the city's labyrinthine streets, seeking out leads and piecing together fragments of information.

As they trudged forward, Sebastian's mind drifted back to Alexander Q, the enigmatic figure who had entrusted them with this peculiar assignment.

In the dimly lit office, Alexander Q sat with a brooding expression, his face shrouded in misery. The room was filled with anticipation as he exuded an aura of power and enigma. Standing tall and commanding attention, his large frame seemed to dominate the space, casting a formidable presence.

Clad in a dark suit that appeared almost like a shadow, Alexander Q wore his attire with an effortless elegance that matched his enigmatic personality. The fabric clung to his broad shoulders, emphasising his stature and giving him an air of authority. The suit was impeccably tailored, symbolising his attention to detail and his penchant for perfection.

His harsh frown etched deep lines on his face, evidence of a life filled with hardship and experiences that weighed heavily on him. Each crease told a story of determination and resilience, as if the world's weight rested on his shoulders. His eyes, concealed beneath the furrowed brow, shimmered with sadness and resolve, reflecting his struggles.

Alexander Q was a man who meant business, and it showed in his every action and demeanour. He had little time for small talk or trivial matters, always focused on the task. His expression rarely softened, revealing a man who had learned to shield his emotions, becoming an impenetrable fortress against the world.

The office had files meticulously prepared, waiting for Sebastian to delve into them. These files represented many business ventures, an intricate web of opportunities and risks that Alexander Q had painstakingly gathered. With every detail meticulously organised, it was clear that he was a man who left no stone unturned.

Despite the presence of the files, Alexander Q hardly spoke. His silence seemed to add to his aura of mystery, leaving those around him wondering about the depths of his knowledge and the secrets he held. He understood the power of restraint, choosing his words carefully and only speaking when necessary.

His silence, however, did not diminish his influence. Those who worked with him knew that his silence carried weight, his approval or disapproval conveyed through a mere nod or a raised eyebrow. His air of mystery only heightened their curiosity, inspiring fear and respect.

Alexander Q was a man of hidden depths and unspoken wisdom. He possessed a wealth of knowledge and experiences that shaped his every move. Behind closed doors, he analysed situations, calculated risks, and strategized his next move.

Through his silent contemplation, he unravelled the intricacies of the business world, making decisions that would impact the lives of many.

Q, the head of their clandestine organisation, was known for his sharp intellect and unwavering dedication to the cause. The weight of his expectations pressed upon Sebastian's shoulders, reminding him of the importance of their task.

The assassinations of three FBI agents and their families in their homes had been devastating. It was a heinous act that had rocked the foundations of law enforcement, shattering the illusion of safety.

But the horror did not end there. In a chilling sequence of events, an aeroplane carrying seven members of the UK's GCHQ had been hacked and subsequently crashed into the vast expanse of the ocean. The magnitude of the tragedy was unimaginable, as the loss of such skilled intelligence operatives dealt a severe blow to national security. Simultaneously, a mysterious and powerful hacker had breached the US CIA and the UK SIS MI5 and MI6 systems, leaving the world's most sophisticated intelligence networks vulnerable and exposed. The scale of the cyber intrusion was unprecedented, raising questions about the capabilities and intentions of the unknown terrorist cell behind it.

The gravity of these events had led investigators like Sebastian to trace the threads of this case to an unknown terrorist cell. This clandestine group had orchestrated a series of attacks, each more audacious than the last, striking fear into the hearts of intelligence agencies worldwide. Their ability to infiltrate highly secure systems and execute deadly missions with precision indicated a level of sophistication that was deeply troubling.

The investigation had become a race against time, a desperate attempt to prevent further attacks and dismantle the shadowy organization orchestrating these events. Sebastian was keenly aware that the safety and security of countless lives hung in the balance. The weight of responsibility pressed upon him as he scrutinized every detail in the files, searching for any leads or patterns that could provide a breakthrough.

The information in the files revealed a complex web of connections, encrypted communications, and clandestine meetings. Sebastian meticulously mapped out the evidence, piecing together the puzzle of the unknown terrorist cell. Each file was a breadcrumb, leading him closer to understanding their motives and identifying the key players involved.

As Sebastian meticulously sifted through the files, his mind absorbed every detail. Each document, photograph, and report contained a piece of the puzzle, and he was determined to uncover the truth hidden within. The room grew silent, save for the rustling of paper as he furrowed his brow, studying the connections and patterns before him.

Sebastian shook off his fatigue with a determined sigh and quickened his pace. Christopher matched his stride, their synchronised footsteps echoing a shared resolve. They were committed to unravelling the truth, no matter the toll it took on their weary

Pushing through their fatigue, Sebastian and Christopher intensified their efforts. They gathered evidence, cross-referenced information, and conducted discreet surveillance where necessary. The puzzle slowly emerged, revealing a network of interconnected businesses involved in money laundering and illegal transactions.

The duo knew they were getting closer to exposing the masterminds behind the operation. The risk grew higher, but so did their resolve. They knew they couldn't afford to falter or let exhaustion compromise their judgement.

Late into the night, they found themselves standing outside the door of a seemingly innocuous storefront. During their investigation, the business had raised some suspicions, and they believed it could be the missing piece that would unravel the entire criminal web. They exchanged a determined look, took a deep breath, and pushed the door open.

They found a maze of hidden rooms, computers, and stacks of incriminating documents. The evidence they had been seeking was right before their eyes. Sebastian and Christopher quickly went to work, meticulously collecting the evidence, taking photographs, and ensuring they left no trace behind.

Their discovery would have far-reaching implications for the criminal network and the innocent individuals unknowingly caught up in its activities. Sebastian and Christopher knew that their efforts would help bring justice to those affected and ensure that the perpetrators faced the consequences of their actions.

As they exited the building, carrying the weight of their findings, the night air felt colder, but the satisfaction of a job well done warmed their spirits. They knew their work wasn't over yet— there would be paperwork, court hearings, and further investigations—but they celebrated a small victory at that moment.

Sebastian Briggs and Christopher Shaw upheld their responsibilities, even in the face of fatigue and adversity. They had followed the path set before them, relentlessly pursued the truth, and made progress in dismantling a criminal network that had plagued their community.

With renewed determination, they walked away from the dimly lit corridor, ready to face the challenges ahead. Their commitment to justice remained unyielding, as they understood that their work would continue to make a difference, one investigation at a time.

Q's assignment had thrust them into a world of shadows and secrets, but they were detectives driven by a sense of justice. No matter how tired they felt or the obstacles they faced, Sebastian Briggs and Christopher Shaw were resolved to see their investigation to its conclusion. The investigation had taken Sebastian Briggs and Christopher Shaw into a dark and secretive world. The weight of the responsibility entrusted to them by Q pressed upon their shoulders, but they remained undeterred. They were detectives driven by a deep-rooted sense of justice, a determination to uncover the truth and bring the perpetrators to light.

Despite how tired they felt, the numerous obstacles, and the complex deceit they encountered, Sebastian and Christopher remained resolute. They knew that the path they had embarked upon was not an easy one, but they were willing to endure the hardships to fulfil their duty.

CHAPTER TWO

Sebastian Briggs, known to his closest acquaintances as Briggs, allowed himself a moment of respite in the comfort of his living room. He was a man of refined taste and meticulous nature and was immersed in the serene ambience of his bachelor's den. The soft glow of a single lamp bathed the room in a subdued light, muting the bold colours and blending the contemporary furnishings seamlessly into an oasis of comfort and elegance.

Seated on the big, plush sofa, Sebastian took in the sight of his carefully curated surroundings. Each piece of furniture, ornament, and decoration had been chosen precisely, reflecting his discerning eye for aesthetics. The room spoke of a man who appreciated the finer things in life, someone who understood the power of creating an atmosphere that captivated the senses.

Sebastian allowed himself to drift into a dreamy state as he savoured the sip of scotch. The smoothness of the amber liquid danced on his palate, providing a momentary respite from the weight of his responsibilities. The subtle aroma of the scotch mingled with the room's fragrance, adding another layer to the sensory experience.

Over the years, Sebastian had carefully amassed a collection of items that exuded elegance and a hint of sensuality. It was an intentional blend designed to intrigue and captivate those who entered his sanctuary. Women were drawn to the room, sensing the allure and danger emanating from its essence.

The room's ambience spoke of comfort and risk, enticing women to tread cautiously. It was an invitation to explore the depths of Sebastian's world, a tantalising glimpse into the complexities that lay within. The room bespoke a man who possessed an enigmatic charm, a man who demanded attention and inspired a mix of curiosity and caution.

Sebastian leaned back against the sofa, immersing himself in his den's tranquillity. The soft music playing in the background added another layer of sophistication, its melodic notes mingling with the subtle sounds of the surrounding city.

At this moment, Sebastian found solace in his carefully crafted haven. The room was not just a collection of furniture and decor; it reflected his essence, a sanctuary that provided him respite from the demanding world outside.

With each sip of scotch, he savoured the symphony of flavours and the warmth that spread through his body. He appreciated the elegance and effect of the room, knowing that it had the power to entice, captivate, and perhaps even warn those who dared to venture further into his world.

Sebastian Briggs, a man of refined taste and hidden depths, revelled in the comfort and allure of his bachelor's den. In this haven of tranquillity, he could momentarily escape the chaos of his profession and find solace in the artistry of his surroundings.

As he sat on the sofa, lost in his thoughts, the past few months' events weighed heavily on his mind. The investigation into the assassination affair had taken a toll on him physically and emotionally. The long nights, the constant danger, and the relentless pursuit of the truth had left him yearning for solace.

He glanced at the clock on the wall, its hands ticking away the minutes. It was late, and the city outside was enveloped in silence, a temporary respite from the chaos that awaited him outside these walls. In this room, he found a sanctuary, a place to momentarily escape the harsh realities of his profession.

Sebastian's eyes wandered around the room, taking in the artwork adorning the walls and the sleek bookshelves displaying his collection of classic literature and espionage novels. It was a space that reflected his multifaceted personality—part gentleman, part warrior.

The sound of footsteps approached, interrupting his reverie. Christopher entered the room, his face marked with fatigue but his eyes still bright with determination. Sebastian acknowledged him with a nod, appreciating his younger colleague's dedication and unwavering loyalty.

Christopher sat opposite Sebastian, glancing around the room with curiosity and admiration. "This place is something else, Sebastian. It's like stepping into another world of sophistication and mystery."

Sebastian chuckled, acknowledging the sentiment. "Yes, it's my little refuge from the chaos of our work. A place where I can momentarily forget the darkness surrounding us and find a semblance of peace."

Christopher leaned back, a contemplative expression on his face. "I often wonder, Sebastian, how do you stay composed amidst all the chaos? The constant danger and uncertainties are enough to drive anyone to the edge."

Sebastian's gaze turned thoughtful, his eyes glinting with a hint of melancholy. "It's not always easy, Christopher. There are moments when the weight of our mission threatens to crush me. But in those moments, I remind myself of the importance of what we do. We're the ones who stand between the innocent and those who seek to harm them. Our work is a necessary sacrifice, as challenging as it may be."

Christopher nodded, absorbing Sebastian's words. He admired his mentor's strength and resilience, the way he carried himself with a sense of purpose. "I suppose you're right, Sebastian. Our duty calls us to venture into the darkness to face the unknown head-on. But in this room, moments like these, where we can find solace and gather the strength to continue."

Sebastian raised his glass, a gesture of camaraderie. "To find solace amidst the chaos, and to never lose sight of the light within us."

They clinked their glasses together, the sound ringing through the room. At that moment, surrounded by elegance and shared understanding, Sebastian and Christopher found a brief respite from the shadows that awaited them outside. It reminded them of their shared purpose and the importance of finding balance in a world consumed by darkness.

The room held its secrets, just like they were determined to unravel the assassination affair. But for now, it offered them a sanctuary, a place to gather strength, and a reminder that they were not alone despite their challenges.

Sebastian Briggs had always valued his privacy and security, understanding the importance of constantly changing locations to stay one step ahead of potential threats. With its unique features and hidden advantages, this apartment had become his haven amid his dangerous profession.

After Christopher left, the bedroom door beckoned, promising a momentary escape from the world outside. Sebastian stood up, his footsteps hushed on the plush carpet as he approached the door. He pushed it open, revealing a tranquil sanctuary adorned with soft, neutral tones and a luxurious bed draped in crisp linens.

He stepped inside, feeling the day's tension begin to melt away. The French doors at the back provided a glimpse of the outside world, allowing a gentle breeze to filter through, carrying a sense of freedom. The room exuded an air of serenity, inviting him to leave behind the worries of his mission and find solace in much-needed rest.

The kitchen door beckoned next, and Sebastian followed its call. He entered a functional, aesthetically pleasing space with state-of-the-art appliances and gleaming countertops. It was where he could indulge in his culinary pursuits, finding solace in the simplicity of preparing a meal.

As Sebastian moved through the apartment, he couldn't help but appreciate the thought and effort he had put into creating this sanctuary. The terrace held a special significance. It was a rare luxury in his line of work—a private outdoor space where he could immerse himself in nature, breathe in fresh air, and momentarily escape the confines of his profession.

Q had initially been reluctant to grant him this apartment with a terrace, concerned about the potential risks it posed. But Sebastian had argued persuasively, emphasising the importance of balance in his life. He had convinced Q that having a space where he could find respite from the demands of his mission would ultimately make him a more effective agent.

As Sebastian stood on the terrace, his eyes taking in the view of the city below, he felt a sense of gratitude. The low stone walls and evergreen planters provided a privacy shield, allowing him to enjoy the outdoors without prying eyes. It was a small slice of tranquillity in a world full of chaos.

At that moment, Sebastian realised the value of these simple pleasures. The apartment was more than just a physical space; it manifested his desire for a semblance of normalcy amidst his extraordinary circumstances. It reminded him that even amid danger and uncertainty, he could create moments of peace and find his own sanctuary.

With renewed appreciation for his surroundings, Sebastian knew he would continue to fight for the truth, unravel the complexities of the assassination affair, and protect those who relied on him. But he also understood the importance of balance, of cherishing the spaces that offered solace and respite.

Sebastian savoured the tranquillity as the evening breeze brushed against his face before stepping back inside, ready to face the challenges that awaited him outside his haven. The apartment had become more than just walls and furniture; it symbolised his resilience and unwavering commitment to his mission.

Racheal came in that evening to see him. The soft melodies of Bossa Nova filled the air, creating a soothing ambience that wrapped around him like a warm embrace. The dim lighting cast a gentle glow, accentuating the allure of the woman by his side.

They had shared a simple dinner; the remnants adorned the coffee table before them. She leaned against him, her presence both captivating and comforting. Her delicate fragrance mingled with the notes of the music, creating an intoxicating blend that enveloped his senses.

Sebastian took a sip of champagne, savouring the effervescence on his tongue. The cool liquid offered a refreshing contrast to the warmth of the room and the company he kept. At this moment, surrounded by the harmonious combination of music, fine wine, and the presence of a captivating woman, he allowed himself to momentarily escape the weight of his mission.

The woman's features were softened in the muted light, her eyes reflecting a mix of tenderness and a hint of mystery. Her presence was a balm to his weary soul, reminding him of the beauty that still existed amidst the chaos of his profession.

Sebastian ran his fingers gently through her hair, relishing the silkiness of each strand. Their physical and emotional connection was a rare and precious bond in his tumultuous life. He found solace and a respite from the relentless pursuit of truth in her arms.

As the Bossa Nova melodies continued filling the room, Sebastian was transported to a different world—a world where danger and uncertainty were momentarily forgotten, replaced by a sense of tranquillity and contentment. In this private sanctuary, he allowed himself to indulge in the pleasures of the present, cherishing the company of the woman who had found her way into his heart.

He raised his glass, a silent toast to the moments of respite that brought balance to his life. In this oasis of calm, I found solace in the simplicity of shared moments and the power of connection.

Rachel's presence beside Briggs was both captivating and comforting. Her tall stature commanded attention, but she carried herself with a grace that belied her height. She embodied his preference for full-figured women, with curves that accentuated her femininity.

Her hair caught the light as a redhead, cascading in waves that shimmered with golden hues. The glow of the room further enhanced her radiant beauty. Her heavy-lashed, languid eyes held a hint of mystery, drawing him in with their depth.

Briggs shifted on the sofa, his feet on the coffee table. He wiggled his toes, feeling a sense of contentment wash over him. The weight of the day's activities had taken its toll on his feet, and he relished the opportunity to let them recover from the afternoon of walking.

The softness of the carpet beneath his bare feet provided a soothing contrast to the rigours of his mission. It was a small indulgence, a simple pleasure that reminded him to take care of himself amidst the demands of his profession.

Briggs glanced at Rachel, a playful smile tugging at the corners of his lips. "You know, Rachel, there's something truly liberating about kicking off your shoes and letting your feet breathe. It's these little moments of comfort that make all the difference."

Rachel chuckled softly, her eyes sparkling with warmth. "I couldn't agree more, Briggs. Sometimes, it's the simplest things that bring us the greatest joy. In a world filled with chaos and danger, it's important to find moments of relaxation and rejuvenation."

Briggs nodded, appreciating her understanding. He leaned back against the cushions, the sound of Bossa Nova creating a soothing backdrop to their conversation. At this moment, he allowed himself to fully immerse in the present, savouring the company of Rachel and the comfort of his own home.

As they sat there, toes wiggling on the coffee table, the weight of their mission momentarily faded into the background. They found solace in each other's presence, a respite from the challenges that awaited them outside those walls.

At that moment, Briggs realised that these simple pleasures—a captivating companion, the softness beneath his feet—reminded him of his humanity. He would continue to fight in the face of danger and darkness but also cherish the moments of comfort and connection that kept him grounded.

With gratitude, Briggs leaned closer to Rachel, their fingers intertwining. In their shared silence, they found a language that surpassed words—a language of understanding, support, and the unspoken promise to face whatever challenges lay ahead.

The room enveloped them in its warmth, and as the Bossa Nova melodies gently faded into the background, Briggs and Rachel embraced the sanctuary they had created.

Sebastian Briggs found himself pulled back into reality, away from the dreamy state he had momentarily indulged in. The words on the page, now blurred by the sudden interruption, reminded him that he had been immersed in a novel, a temporary escape from the demands of his profession.

He glanced at his surroundings, the room he had carefully curated to reflect his tastes and desires. The elegance and allure that had captivated him before now seemed distant, overshadowed by the urgency of his mission. The thought of the impending danger and the investigation that awaited him tugged at his consciousness, reminding him of his responsibilities.

Sebastian set the book aside, its pages whispering a promise to return him to another world. But for now, the words would have to wait. Duty called, and he couldn't afford to lose himself in fiction while facing real-world challenges.

As he rose from the sofa, he cast one last look at the room, appreciating its aesthetic appeal but knowing it held no answers to the mysteries he had to unravel. The allure of the space, once a refuge from the complexities of his profession, now paled compared to the importance of his mission.

With determination etched on his face, Sebastian left the room, stepping into the unknown again. The world outside held its own allure and dangers, its stories waiting to be uncovered. And as he ventured forth, he carried with him the memory of the room—a reminder of the balance between the allure of comfort and the call of duty, a symbol of the respite he sought but knew he couldn't afford for long.

Sebastian Briggs stepped into the darkness, ready to face the challenges ahead. With its elegance and sensuality, the room remained behind a silent witness to his choices and a beacon of solace for when he would return, seeking a momentary escape from the realities of his world.

He got a text from Racheal at that moment. 'Shit!' he looked around. Tonight was date night with Racheal. This realisation had skipped his mind because of his mission. That evening, he was to meet up with Christopher at Tony Al Garfhr's shop, The city's infamous gun dealer. Racheal was one not to take no for an answer, so he knew there was no escaping this night. *Dinner's still at your place, right?* Racheal had texted him. Briggs hesitated and texted back *Sure* and turned around.

That evening Racheal arrived in Sebastian's quaint apartment. A sense of warmth and intimacy filled the air as he prepared for a date night with Rachel. The soft glow of candlelight casts a romantic ambience, creating the perfect setting for an evening of connection and shared moments.

Sebastian, though reluctant, had taken great care in planning the evening, wanting to create an experience that would be memorable for both. He ordered a simmering spaghetti sauce that filled the apartment with its mouth-watering aroma. The tantalising scent wafted through the air, tempting their senses and setting the stage for a delightful culinary experience.

Racheal had taken great care in selecting her attire for the evening, wanting to look her best for this special occasion. She entered the apartment, her sparkling presence immediately catching Sebastian's eye.

Rachel wore a stunning body-con glitter dress that accentuated her every curve. The dress shimmered in the soft lighting, glowing radiantly around her. The fabric clung to her figure elegantly, showcasing her confidence and femininity. It was a dress that spoke volumes about her sense of style and desire to make this evening special.

Her fiery red hair was gathered in a sleek ponytail, allowing her beautiful features to take centre stage. As she moved, her hair swayed gently, adding an element of playfulness to her overall appearance. The crimson-red hue of her lips matched perfectly with the rest of her ensemble, exuding a touch of boldness and sophistication.

Sebastian couldn't help but be captivated by Rachel's beauty as she stood before him. He greeted her with a warm smile and a gentle embrace, appreciating her effort to make this night extraordinary. Their connection was immediate, and the energy between them crackled with excitement.

They made their way to the elegantly set table, where a bottle of their favourite wine awaited them. Sebastian poured the deep red liquid into their glasses, the rich aroma filling the air. They clinked their glasses together, a silent toast to the moments they were about to share.

As they settled into their seats, conversation flowed effortlessly. Their words danced in the air, carrying stories, laughter, and glimpses into their lives. They spoke of dreams and aspirations, moments that had shaped them, and the bond that continued to grow between them.

Sebastian served the spaghetti, the aroma of the sauce intensifying their hunger. The flavours danced on their tongues, each bite celebrating their culinary adventure. Sharing a meal became a moment of connection as they fed each other small bites, their eyes locked in a gaze that conveyed more than words ever could.

As the night progressed, the atmosphere became infused with intimacy and tenderness. They moved to the living room, where the soft glow of candlelight bathed them in a warm embrace. Their bodies found comfort in each other's presence as they curled up on the couch, the air thick with shared laughter and stolen glances.

Sebastian brushed a strand of Rachel's hair away from her face, his gentle touch filled with affection. Their fingers intertwined, and the world outside ceased to exist at that moment.

In an instant, the moment's tranquillity was shattered by a deafening bang reverberating through Sebastian's apartment. The sound of the door being forcefully struck sent shockwaves through the air, immediately triggering Sebastian's instincts. With lightning-fast reflexes, he reacted without hesitation, swiftly pushing Rachel to the floor and positioning himself on top of her as a human shield.

The room erupted in chaos as bullets tore through the walls, shattering the serene atmosphere that had enveloped them moments ago. The once serene and cosy space was now transformed into a battleground, with the staccato rhythm of gunfire echoing through the air. The sound was ear-piercing, the intensity of the situation threatening to drown out all other senses.

Huddled together in a corner, Rachel's heart raced, her mind racing to make sense of the terror unfolding before her eyes. Sebastian's protective embrace offered solace amidst the chaos, but fear still coursed through their veins.

As bullets continued to rain down upon them, Sebastian's sharp mind kicked into overdrive. Amidst the chaos, he strained to detect the origin of the sniper's attack. His senses heightened, and his trained eyes scanned the room, searching for clues that might reveal the assailant's location. It was a race against time, as every passing moment increased the risk to their lives.

Sebastian spotted a telltale glint through the window, a fleeting glimpse of the sniper's presence. It became clear that their assailant had taken a position outside the apartment, utilising the window as a strategic entry point. The vulnerability of their once-secure sanctuary ignited a fire within Sebastian's heart, a fierce determination to protect Rachel and eliminate the threat that jeopardised their lives.

With Rachel still sheltered beneath his protective embrace, Sebastian knew they needed to act swiftly and decisively. Their survival depended on their ability to outmanoeuvre their unseen enemy and regain control of the situation. Every move had to be calculated, every action deliberate, as they sought to turn the tide in their favour.

As the barrage of bullets momentarily subsided, Sebastian recognized the need to create a diversion to disrupt the sniper's focus and gain the upper hand. With a steely resolve, he devised a plan during the chaos. With one swift motion, he reached for an object within reach—a strategically placed bookshelf—and sent it crashing to the ground, creating a cacophony of noise and distraction.

The crash reverberated through the room, momentarily disorienting their assailant and disrupting their aim. It was the split-second opportunity they needed to escape the line of fire. Keeping Rachel close, Sebastian propelled them towards the nearest exit, their bodies moving in sync, guided by a shared survival instinct.

They cautiously navigated the room, utilising the furniture as cover, darting from one point of concealment to another. Every step carried the weight of their lives, their bodies pressed against the walls, seeking refuge from the deadly onslaught. The adrenaline coursing through their veins fuelled their agility and focus as they moved with a sense of urgency and purpose.

He scanned their surroundings, his trained eyes keenly attuned to every detail, searching for the most viable route to safety. While he did that, his gaze caught the men carefully stepping inside. He and Racheal quickly ducked behind the sofa, hiding from their reach. He reached out to his jacket to get his gun.

Sebastian Briggs cursed under his breath as his hand grasped nothing but air. The realisation hit him hard. He had left his gun behind, opting for a peaceful evening with Rachel instead of carrying the weight of steel on his person. At that moment, he regretted his decision.

With his heart pounding in his chest, Sebastian strained to hear any sign of movement or the approaching footsteps of his assailants. The room was filled with tense silence, broken only by the faint sound of Rachel's steady breathing. He knew he couldn't remain a sitting target for long.

Gritting his teeth, Sebastian made a split-second decision. He pushed on Rachel's shoulder, signalling her to stay low and safe. Then, he slowly raised his head, peering around the sofa's edge to assess the situation.

Two men stood near the terrace doors, their guns held firmly in their hands. One was tall and thin, with a tight mouth and twitching eyelids—a nervous type. The other was of medium height, muscular, and exuded an air of strength—a formidable opponent.

Sebastian's mind raced, analysing his options. He needed to neutralise the threat and protect Rachel. Without a weapon, his physical prowess and quick thinking were his only allies.

Tightening his leg muscles, Sebastian crouched low, gathering leverage and summoning his strength. In one swift motion, he propelled himself over the sofa, his body colliding with both men as they stood close together. The impact caused the more petite man to lose his grip on his gun, which clattered to the carpeted floor.

Sebastian's instincts took over as he fought fiercely with the taller man. He used his training, employing precise strikes and leveraging his weight to gain an advantage. Their bodies writhed on the floor, each vying for control.

Sebastian redoubled his efforts as the man's hand slithered toward the fallen gun, delivering a final forceful blow that sent the assailant sprawling. He wasted no time, seizing the opportunity to disarm him entirely and ensure his temporary incapacitation.

Breathing heavily, Sebastian turned to the remaining threat—the more petite man who had lost his weapon. He scanned the room, searching for any makeshift weapon that could aid him in subduing the assailant and preventing further danger.

His eyes fell upon the champagne cooler sitting on the coffee table. Without hesitation, he lunged toward it, snatching the heavy container and wielding it as an improvised weapon.

Bracing himself, Sebastian prepared to confront the remaining attacker, knowing that his determination and resourcefulness were his best chances of surviving this deadly encounter and protecting Rachel at all costs.

A quick vision of the gun resting in his bureau drawer flashed to mind as Sebastian cursed under his breath. He had chosen to leave the gun behind, considering the evening's plans with Rachel. The last thing he wanted was to introduce a weapon that could disrupt their intimacy.

Sebastian quickly assessed the situation, mentally categorising the attackers. He knew he had to act swiftly and decisively to protect himself and Rachel. Tightening his leg muscles and crouching for leverage, he launched himself over the sofa, aiming to strike both men simultaneously since they had foolishly remained close together.

The impact of his weight caused the more petite man to lose his grip on his gun, which thudded onto the carpeted floor. Sensing an opportunity, the taller man made a break for the open door, attempting to escape.

Sebastian reacted without hesitation, seizing the moment. He tackled the man beneath him, their bodies crashing to the ground. Aware of the danger posed by the fallen gun, he intensified his efforts, pressing down harder on the assailant and impeding his reach. Assessing the man's physique, Sebastian noted his rugged and muscular build, devoid of excess weight.

With every ounce of his strength, Sebastian prevented the man from reclaiming the weapon. He used his body as a barrier, pushing against the man's movements and maintaining control. His training and experience came into play as he utilised his knowledge of close combat to maintain the upper hand.

Breathing heavily, Sebastian knew his confrontation with the remaining attacker wasn't over. He still had to deal with the more petite man who had lost his gun. Assessing the room for available makeshift weapons, he quickly spotted a heavy object—a champagne cooler on the coffee table.

Seizing the cooler, Sebastian prepared to face the second assailant, his determination unwavering. He understood that his resourcefulness and adaptability would be crucial in navigating this dangerous encounter and ensuring his and Rachel's safety.

Terrace. Briggs's mind raced as he assessed the situation. He knew he couldn't let them escape.

Gritting his teeth against the pain throbbing in his temple, he summoned every ounce of determination and gave chase.

Briggs propelled himself forward with adrenaline, his feet pounding against the stone surface. He weaved through the low walls that divided the apartments, closing the distance between himself and the fleeing assailants. The situation's urgency heightened as he knew he had to apprehend them before they disappeared into the night.

The moonlight cast shadows on the path ahead, guiding his pursuit. As Briggs neared the end of the terrace, he could hear their footsteps fading. He couldn't let them slip away. Summoning his last energy reserves, he pushed himself to run faster, his heart pounding.

Just as the distance between them seemed insurmountable, Briggs saw a glimmer of hope. The two men had reached a wrought-iron gate that led to the street below. They fumbled with the latch, their desperation palpable.

Briggs propelled himself forward with a final burst of speed. He lunged, reaching out with his hand, and grabbed the taller man's coat. The fabric slipped through his fingers, leaving Briggs grasping at the air.

But he wasn't about to give up. Determination surged through his veins as he closed in on them. With a surge of strength, he launched towards the gate, grabbing the bars and swinging his body through the opening. He landed with a thud on the pavement, adrenaline fuelling his every move.

Briggs's vision focused on the retreating figures. He saw them sprinting down the street, their forms growing smaller in the distance. He gritted his teeth, his mind racing to devise a plan. He couldn't let them disappear into the night.

As he started to give chase once more, Briggs spotted a nearby parked car. Inspiration struck him, and he sprinted towards it. He fumbled with the door, his hands shaking from the adrenaline coursing through his veins. Finally, he managed to open it and jumped into the driver's seat.

Without hesitation, Briggs turned the key in the ignition, the engine roaring to life. He slammed his foot on the gas pedal and peeled out onto the street, the tires screeching in protest.

With the car's speed and unwavering determination, Briggs closed the distance between himself and the fleeing assailants. He could see the fear in their eyes as they glanced back, realising their escape was being cut short.

Briggs's grip tightened on the steering wheel as he prepared to intercept them. His mind raced with calculations, timing his moves precisely. As he neared the two men, he swerved the car, aiming to cut them off.

The car collided with the fleeing figures, sending them sprawling onto the pavement. The impact was inevitable. Briggs brought the vehicle to a screeching halt, the scent of burning rubber filling the air.

Taking a moment to collect himself, Briggs stepped out of the car, his heart pounding. He approached the two men, their faces etched with pain and defeat. They had underestimated him, and now they would face the consequences.

As he stood over them, Briggs knew this encounter was far from over. The events of the evening had taken an unexpected turn, and he had to unravel the mysteries beneath the surface.

Briggs returned to his house, determined to protect himself and Rachel. Briggs took a deep breath, steeling himself for the challenges ahead. He met Racheal, who still looked shocked and disoriented, emerging from behind the couch. 'What...who were those men?!' Racheal managed to screech from her mouth.
'Distance yourself from this. It's for the best," Briggs replied, his voice tinged with regret. He understood Rachel's fear and confusion and didn't want to put her in any more danger. Racheal quickly grabbed her purse and her jacket as she prepared to leave.

Briggs watched as Rachel hurriedly prepared to leave. He couldn't shake off the feeling of disappointment and frustration. The events of the evening had taken an unexpected turn, and now he had to deal with the aftermath alone.

As Rachel approached the door, Briggs couldn't help but feel a pang of sadness. He hoped their evening together would be different, filled with warmth and intimacy. But circumstances had forced them into a dangerous situation, and now their paths seemed to diverge. Briggs called out to her, his voice filled with genuine concern. "Take care, Rachel. Be safe. If you ever need me, you know where to find me."

He walked to the bedroom and retrieved his gun from the bureau drawer. The weapon's weight felt reassuring in his hand, a reminder of the dangers he faced. With a sigh, he tucked it back into his coat, ready to face whatever lay ahead.

She paused for a moment, her eyes meeting him briefly. Her gaze had a mix of emotions—fear, uncertainty, and a flicker of something else. But she didn't respond. With a determined look, she opened the door and stepped out into the night, leaving Briggs behind.

Turning back to the room, Briggs glanced around, taking in the remnants of the chaos. The split contents of the coffee table, the damaged furniture, and the bullet holes in the walls were stark reminders of the violence that had unfolded. He knew he couldn't stay here for long. He needed to regroup, gather information, and find out who was behind the attack.

Briggs's mind raced with questions. Who were those men? Why were they after him? And what did they want? He knew he had to uncover the truth and protect himself from further harm. But first, he needed to find a safe place to gather his thoughts and plan his next move.

Alone in the room, Briggs took a deep breath and focused his mind. He had to uncover the truth and stay one step ahead of his enemies. As he walked towards the door, his footsteps echoed in the empty space, a reminder of the challenges that awaited him in the dark and dangerous world he inhabited.

CHAPTER THREE

Briggs and Christopher Shaw found themselves in the early morning. The sun still lingered below the horizon, casting a faint glow that struggled to penetrate the dense fog blanketing the city.

As they made their way through the dimly lit streets, the air was heavy with an eerie stillness. The familiar sights of bustling London had faded into the background, replaced by dilapidated buildings and neglected alleyways. The urban decay was evident, with graffiti-covered walls and broken windows as a stark reminder of the hardship in the neighbourhood.

The darkness seemed to seep into every crevice, wrapping around the derelict structures like a cloak of shadows. Streetlights, few and far between, flickered weakly, casting feeble beams that struggled to penetrate the thick fog that clung to the air. It was as if the city held its breath, waiting for the first rays of dawn to break through the oppressive gloom.

The buildings stood tall, but their facades were weathered and worn, bearing the scars of neglect and hardship. Crumbling brickwork and cracked pavements lined the desolate streets, depicting abandonment and despair. Trash littered the sidewalks, remnants of a community forgotten by the world outside.

As Briggs and Shaw ventured deeper into the heart of this desolate neighbourhood, the sense of isolation grew. It was a place where poverty and crime thrived, where hope struggled to find a foothold amidst the shadows. The silence was punctuated only by distant sirens and the occasional echo of footsteps in the distance, creating an ominous symphony that underscored the danger that lurked in the darkness.

The fog, a spectral presence, hung like a heavy veil. It clung to every surface, obscuring visibility and distorting shapes into amorphous figures. The world felt muted and surreal as if reality had been diluted in the mist. Each step forward was met with uncertainty as the fog enveloped Briggs and

Shaw, concealing their movements and heightening their vigilance.

The dim light of the impending sunrise struggled against the thick fog, casting an ethereal glow that danced on the edges of perception. The world's colours seemed muted and faded as if drained by the oppressive atmosphere. Shadows morphed and shifted with each passing moment, playing tricks on the senses and heightening the tension that gripped Briggs and Shaw.

The scent of dampness hung in the air, mingling with the faint odours of decay and desperation. It was a stark reminder of the hardships endured by those who called this dark ghetto home. The echoes of past struggles reverberated through the streets, whispering tales of resilience and resilience against all odds.

As Briggs and Shaw navigated the labyrinthine alleys and narrow passages, they remained on high alert, every sense attuned to the dangers that lurked in the shadows. Their footsteps were hushed, their movements deliberate, as they followed the faint trail of clues that led them deeper into the heart of the darkness.

With each passing minute, the anticipation grew as the first rays of sunlight fought through the fog, piercing the shroud that had cloaked the city. The world began to awaken, and the veil of darkness slowly receded, revealing the stark reality of the forgotten ghetto.

Their purpose was to locate Tony Al Garfhr, the notorious gun dealer believed to be responsible for supplying the weapon used in the assassination of an FBI agent and the attempted assassination of Briggs and Rachel the previous night. Determined to bring Tony to justice, Briggs intended to confront him at his apartment, catching him off guard in the early morning hours and gaining an opportunity for interrogation.

Every step taken in the dark ghetto demanded caution and awareness. Briggs and Christopher moved silently, their senses heightened, attuned to any sound or movement that could signal danger. Their footsteps fell softly on the uneven pavement, blending with the hushed whispers of the night as if the city itself held its breath, aware of the gravity of its mission.

The tension in the air was palpable as they approached Tony Al Garfhr's apartment building up the stairs. It stood like a monolithic sentinel amidst the decay, its cracked facade a testament to the secrets it held within. The entrance was guarded by a heavy metal door, its paint long worn away, revealing layers of rust. A sense of anticipation gripped Briggs as he reached for the stairs, the cold metal chilling his hand.

Briggs and Christopher ascended the staircase, each step a calculated movement towards their objective. The worn carpeting whispered beneath their feet, muffling the sound of their progress. The air grew heavier as if the weight of the neighbourhood's hardships had settled into the walls, seeping into every corner.

Reaching the designated floor, they approached Tony's apartment with trepidation and determination. Briggs knew that a confrontation with the infamous gun dealer would not be without risks, but his unwavering dedication to justice propelled him forward.

Briggs paused outside Tony's door, his hand resting on the cool surface. The moment hung in the air, charged with the gravity of the situation. With a steadying breath, he turned the doorknob, which was locked. After several attempts in trying to get it open, Briggs stood back.

Christopher looked through the window to see if they were anyone inside. The room beyond remained cloaked in darkness. The soft rays of dawn filtered through the window, casting a faint glow that gradually dispelled the shadows.

The room revealed signs of a hasty departure as if its occupant had anticipated their arrival. However, the scent of stale tobacco and lingering desperation lingered. The sparse furnishings reflected a life lived on the fringes.

As Briggs and Shaw stood before Tony Al Garfhr's apartment, their anticipation morphed into disappointment when they received no response to their persistent knocking. Each rap on the door echoed through the stillness of the neighbourhood, disturbing the fragile peace that had settled over the early morning hours.

The sound of their repeated knocks reverberated through the quiet streets, interrupting the slumber of the neighbourhood. Curtains twitched, and cautious eyes peered through half-opened blinds, curiosity piqued by the unusual commotion that disturbed the usual tranquillity of the hour. Faces appeared at windows, their expressions a mix of annoyance and intrigue as they sought to discern the source of the disturbance.

The dim glow of streetlights cast fleeting shadows on the faces that emerged from the surrounding buildings. Some residents, clad in dishevelled attire, rubbed their eyes and yawned, questioning the disruption to their sleep. Others, more accustomed to the rhythms of the neighbourhood, cast suspicious glances towards the unfamiliar figures standing before Tony Al Garfhr's apartment.

Whispers filled the air and carried on the gentle breeze that rustled through the narrow alleyways. Speculation and conjecture swirled among the inhabitants, their voices hushed but filled with curiosity. The neighbourhood had its secrets, its unspoken code of conduct, and the arrival of Briggs and Shaw, accompanied by the persistent knocking, defied the unspoken rules of the night.

Some shook their heads dismissively, returning to their beds resignedly, accepting the transient nature of such disturbances. Others, fuelled by a thirst for knowledge or a natural inclination towards voyeurism, lingered at their windows, their gazes fixed on the two figures that represented a disturbance in the tightly woven fabric of their community.

Briggs and Shaw, aware of their unwittingly drawn attention, maintained their composure, their eyes scanning the windows and doorways for any sign of Tony Al Garfhr's presence.

The air was heavy with expectation, as if the very essence of the neighbourhood held its breath, waiting for the resolution that seemed tantalisingly close. Time seemed to stretch, the silence stretching thin as the minutes ticked. The onlookers, drawn by the allure of the unknown, held their breath in unison, hoping to catch a glimpse of the elusive Tony Al Garfhr.

But as the seconds turned into minutes, it became evident that their target remained elusive, his absence a testament to his cunning and ability to evade capture. The disappointment within Briggs and Shaw mingled with the growing impatience of the spectators, who yearned for closure for a resolution to the disturbance that had awakened them from their slumber.

With a shared glance, Briggs and Shaw acknowledged that their search for Tony Al Garfhr would have to continue elsewhere. As Briggs and Shaw were about to leave, their mission seemingly thwarted by Tony Al Garfhr's absence, a door creaked open nearby.

It was a short black woman with a petite frame. Her presence cast a fresh wave of curiosity among the onlookers. Clad in a worn-out robe, her eyes bleary with sleep, she approached the two men cautiously, her voice tinged with concern and curiosity.

She stood before Briggs and Shaw, her appearance reflecting the early hour and her unanticipated encounter. Her dishevelled afro, adorned with a few loose strands that had escaped her attempts to tame them, hinted at a restless night's sleep. She wore a comfortable yet slightly worn-out grey sweater, its fabric hugging her frame with a sense of familiarity.

A knitted scarf, woven in a pattern of black and white, was wrapped snugly around her neck, providing warmth and a touch of character to her ensemble. The scarf bore evidence of its frequent use, displaying faint signs of wear, but it retained a certain charm that suggested Lainy's appreciation for handmade treasures.

"What's all this commotion about at such an ungodly hour?" the woman asked, her voice full of annoyance, yet tempered with genuine interest. Her presence commanded attention, her petite frame imbued with a resolute determination.

Her countenance was marked by a frown etched across her face since she felt irritated at being disturbed in the early morning. Her dark, expressive eyes held a glimmer of defiance.

Briggs, recognizing the inquisitiveness in her eyes, decided to offer a brief explanation. "We apologise for disturbing the peace, ma'am. We are detectives, and we were hoping to locate Tony Al Garfhr, the gun dealer connected to recent criminal activities. We believed he resided in this building."

Her eyebrows furrowed, her eyes narrowing as she absorbed the information. The mention of Tony Al Garfhr seemed to stir something within her, a flicker of recognition and concern. She glanced around, the onlookers hanging onto every word, their collective interest piqued by the revelation.

"Tony Al Garfhr, you say?" She muttered, her voice tinged with a mix of apprehension and caution. "He's not around. Hasn't been for a few days." As she spoke, her voice carried a mixture of weariness and determination, the weariness from her sleep disturbance.

Brigg turned around fully to her. 'We are so sorry to disturb you, ma'am. Might we know, ma'am?'

'The name is Elaine Michael. But people around here know me as Lainy.'

'Okay, Lainy, we're looking for Tony Al Garfhr. Are you aware of his whereabouts?'

'I just told you, Mr He moved out quite some time ago. Tony doesn't live here anymore.'

Briggs leaned forward. 'Do you happen to know when he left?'

Elain furrowed her brow. 'Hmm, that will be about a month now.'

'A month? That can't be right.' Briggs looked taken aback.

'Did he leave any forwarding address or mention where he was heading?' Christopher stepped forwards and asked.

'None that I'm aware of. His exit was sudden. One day he was here, and the next, he was gone. The neighbourhood hasn't been the same since.' Elain maintained her straight scrutinising face.

'Did anyone else move in after Tony left? Any new faces around here?' Christopher continued.

'Yes, there have been some new occupants. Well, just one. She strikes me as sinister the first time she steps into Tony's flat.

Briggs paused at Lainy's mention of a new woman. 'Wait, did you say there's someone new living in Tony's flat? A woman?

'Yes, that's correct.' Elain nodded. 'After Tony left, a woman moved in. The neighbours have been talking about her. She's tall, beautiful, with blue eyes. Quite the contrast to Tony, I must say.

Shaw raised an eyebrow. 'Do you know anything about her? Is she Tony's sister or related to him in any way?'

'No, they don't look anything alike.' Elain shook her head. 'There's been speculation, but no one really knows for sure. She keeps to herself mostly, and there's an air of mystery around her.'

Briggs and Christopher contemplated this.

'Well, she's one to carry weapons and use them anytime. That's why these horny bastards stay away from her.'

'Weapons? What kind of weapons' Briggs raised his head.

'Well, Guns with silencers. I've heard her use them. Heard strange noises.' Elain said almost in a whisper. She suddenly seemed nervous as she said this.

"Lainy, I appreciate your response, but we must understand what happened here. Can you provide any more details about this woman? And what made you think those noises were gunshots with silencers?" Brigg asked, his tone firm but not accusatory.

Elain looked slightly taken aback by the questions but quickly composed herself and responded, "I'm sorry, Mr....'

'Briggs'

'Mr Briggs. I don't know the woman, but she seemed agitated and rushed. As for the noises, they were muffled and repetitive, like soft pops. I've watched enough movies to recognise the sound of gunshots with silencers. It scared me, so I came to check on you."

Brigg listened intently, weighing her words and gestures for any signs of deception. Though he found her explanation plausible, he maintained a healthy dose of scepticism. "Fair enough, Lainy.

Elain nodded, her nervous twining and untwining hands resuming. "Yes'

Brigg cautiously moved away from the door, ensuring he kept an eye on Elain while he examined the surroundings for any signs of the woman or any other potential threats. He remained prepared for unforeseen developments, his senses heightened and his grip on the concealed gun steady.

'Lainy, do you know where we might find this woman?' Christopher resumed his questioning.

Elain looked at Christopher with a glare. She seems to be growing irritated. 'Look, I told you she's mysterious. No one knows much about her. She seems to come and go without anyone noticing. It's like she's always slipping in and out unnoticed by the neighbours.'

Briggs raised an eyebrow. 'But surely someone must have seen her leaving or returning to the flat?'

Lainy: (crossing her arms) I'm telling you, it's like she's a ghost. People have tried to watch her, but she's evasive. There have been sightings of her leaving at odd hours, but no one can pinpoint her exact routine or where she goes.'

'We need to gather more information about her movements and activities. She could be key in unravelling the truth behind Tony's operations.' Briggs said firmly to Christopher.

Shaw turned to Elain. 'We appreciate your cooperation, Lainy. We'll take your advice to heart and proceed with caution. Your insights have been invaluable to our investigation.' he said reassuringly.

A figure had been observing them from his window, listening intently to their discussion. Mr Scarlette, a tall Jamaican man with light skin, decided it was time to join the conversation and shed some light on the matter.

Mr Scarlette made his way down the creaking staircase of his apartment building, his steps deliberate and purposeful. His grey, straight hair hung loosely around his face, adorned with beads that had lost some of their lustrs over the years, perhaps due to his smoking habit. His eyes, bloodshot and weary, held a hint of curiosity as he approached the group.

As he emerged from the shadows, the trio fell silent, the attention shifting towards him. Mr Scarlette stood tall, his presence commanding yet non-threatening. He wore a worn-out jacket that had seen better days, and his teeth were artificial and plastic-looking.

Briggs eyed Mr Scarlette with curiosity. 'Can we help you, sir?'

'excuse me for eavesdropping, but I couldn't help but overhear your conversation. Seems like you're all looking for answers, eh?' Mr Scarlette, in a raspy yet friendly voice, said.

Shaw nodded. 'That's correct. We require information on Tony Al Garfhr's activities, and any information would be valuable.

'Well, I can't say I know much about Tony, but I've seen that woman you're talking' about. She ain't your regular neighbour, that's for sure.' Mr Scarlette said, leaning against the wall

Briggs and Christopher's gaze remained on Mr Scarlette curiously.

'Well, Gentlemen, allow me to introduce myself. I'm Mr Scarlette. Please, don't pay too much mind to what Elain was saying. She has a strained relationship with the new neighbours in this neighbourhood. Betty Carter. And she's as lovely as a dove. God knows what a pretty flower like that doing here in our neighbourhood."

Briggs and Christopher exchanged a curious glance.

'Her name is Brett Carter. Is that correct?" Briggs asked

Mr. Scarlette nodded. "That's right, Brett Carter. She's a rather pleasant person, contrary to what some might say. Elain and a few others around here have difficulty getting along with the new faces in our community."

"So you believe that Brett Carter is not involved in any suspicious activities?" Christopher asked

"Absolutely. Brett is a kind and caring individual. I've seen her interact with other neighbours, offering a helping hand and lending a sympathetic ear. Sometimes, misunderstandings can lead to unfounded rumours," Mr Scarlette said, avoiding Lainy's long, lingering, surprised gaze. Elain made to speak, but Briggs interrupted.

"But what about the reports of her carrying weapons and behaving suspiciously?"

Mr Scarlette raised an eyebrow. "Ah, rumours can take on a life of their own, my friends. I wouldn't put too much stock in them. People can often jump to conclusions without having all the facts.

Brett might have her reasons for certain behaviours, but that doesn't necessarily make her a threat."

Mr Scarlette paused for a while as if contemplating his words before he continued.

'Well, she keeps to herself mostly. I ain't gonna lie that sometimes it feels there's something about her that's off. I've seen her in the early morning, heading out when most folks are still sleeping. And her eyes, bloodshot like she's seen things most people wouldn't want to.' Mr Scarlette paused, his gaze distant.

'Do you know where she might be going or what she's involved in?' Briggs pressed

'It's hard to say, my friend. But if I were to guess, I'd say she's got connections in some shady business, just like Tony. Seen here meeting' with suspicious characters down by the old warehouse near the docks. I think she's a little lost girl trying to find her way in the world and mixing herself up with these individuals.' Mr Scarlette said, rubbing his chin.

Shaw took notes. 'That's valuable information, Mr Scarlette. We appreciate your insight. Do you know anything else that could help us in our investigation?'

Mr Scarlette leaned closer, lowering his voice. 'Keep an eye out for her acquaintances. She moves in circles you don't want to mess with. Still, she is a good girl. I know that. I know that. She's just out there protecting herself from the horny bastards in these streets.'

'You mean Horny Bastards like you, Yeh, Scarlette, ' Elain growled at Mr |Scarlette. She didn't look pleased with him.

'Oh, get off my lane, you bloody bitch. You're just jealous of the pretty woman showing up here. At least no one cares about your ass anymore.'

'Oh, they do, you perverted twisted fool. These officers of the Law are out here to serve justice, and here you are, diverting them from justice. You fuckin whore.'

'Oh, I'm the whore? Don't come out here cussin' me in the early hours, woman…I'm here for you, woman.'

As Elaine and Mr Scarlette engaged in a heated argument, their voices filled the air with tension and frustration. The exchange of words escalated, with insults hurled back and forth, each defending their perspective.

Sensing the need to diffuse the situation, Christopher stepped in between the two, his calm demeanour serving as a catalyst for a momentary ceasefire.

"Alright, alright! Let's take a step back here. We're all invested in finding the truth, but arguing won't get us anywhere. Mr Scarlette, we appreciate your insights, and Lainy, we value your concerns. Can you stop the fighting now?"

Elain and Mr Scarlette took a moment to catch their breath, their eyes locked defiantly.

Briggs, who had been contemplating what Mr Scarlette said, raised his raise to Mr Scarlette. "You mentioned that Brett usually returns home in the evening or the early hours of the morning. So, there's a chance she could arrive at any moment?"

Mr. Scarlette nodded. "That's right, my friend. Brett keeps unconventional hours, but she tends to be around during those times. If you're looking to meet her, you might have to be patient and keep an eye out."

"Don't think for a second that I'll change my mind about her. I've seen things and won't be swayed by pretty words." Elainwho was still visibly upset, said Mr Scarlette. It was clear that their fight was far from over.

"Lainy, we understand your concerns and take them seriously. Our objective is to gather all the facts and make an informed judgement. Let's give it some time and see how things unfold."

Lainy's expression softened slightly, yet her scepticism remained apparent. The tension in the air hung thick.

"We appreciate your cooperation, Mr Scarlette. We'll keep a watchful eye and await Brett's return." Briggs said to Mr Scarlette

With a nod of understanding, Mr Scarlette acknowledged Briggs' words.
As they left the scene, the uncertain atmosphere of the dark London ghetto seemed to intensify. The mystery surrounding Brett Carter and the conflicting narratives only added to the enigma they sought to unravel.

They descended the stairs, and as they got to the bottom, they saw a figure in a hood walking up the road. But as the figure spotted them, it quickly crossed the road to the other side.

Briggs and Christopher exchanged a quick glance, their eyes fixed on the hooded figure as she swiftly crossed the street, disappearing into the shadows of the London ghetto. With a shared sense of urgency, they instinctively knew that apprehending this figure could hold crucial answers to their investigation.

Without hesitation, they picked up their pace and closed the distance between themselves and the fleeing figure. 'Stop!' they both said, but the figure took off and ran across the street. Their footsteps echoed through the quiet streets as they pursued her, determined to uncover the truth.

"Briggs, we can't let her slip away. She could be Betty. We need to catch up!"

"I'm right behind you, Christopher!"

As they sprinted through the dimly lit alleys, their focus sharpened, blocking out the surrounding dilapidated buildings and the misty morning air. The hooded figure weaved in and out of sight, expertly manoeuvring through narrow passages, making it challenging for Briggs and Christopher to maintain a clear line of sight.

With every twist and turn, their adrenaline surged, propelling them forward. Their footsteps echoed against the worn cobblestone pavement, the sound a testament to their determination and pursuit of the truth.

"She's fast, Briggs! We need to corner her somehow, cut off her escape route." Christopher stopped while Briggs caught up with him

Briggs bowed, a little exhausted as he tried to catch his breath. "Keep your eyes peeled, Christopher. Look for any opportunity to intercept her. We can't let her disappear into the labyrinth of this neighbourhood."

They took off again. The hooded figure momentarily hesitated as they approached a junction, scanning her surroundings for an escape route. Briggs seized the moment and made a split-second decision, taking a sharp turn down a narrow alley that would intersect the woman's path.

Their hearts raced as they closed in on the hooded figure. Their breaths became ragged, each stride bringing them closer to a possible breakthrough. At that moment, they were propelled by determination, curiosity, and the pursuit of justice.

"Stop! We need to talk! We just want to ask you a few questions!" Briggs yelled, almost out of breath

The woman glanced back, her eyes wide with fear and uncertainty. It was evident that she knew they were onto her. Without a word, she quickened her pace, her desperate attempts to evade capture intensifying.

Christopher: "We can't let her get away, Briggs! We're so close!"

Briggs and Christopher pushed themselves to the limits, closing the gap between them and the fleeing woman. Their pursuit led them through a maze of narrow streets, where the surrounding buildings cast long shadows, further adding to the suspense of the chase.

Briggs and Christopher pressed on, their determination unyielding, as they pursued the figure through the labyrinthine streets. Their breaths came in ragged gasps, their muscles burning with exertion. Yet, the figure seemed to possess an uncanny ability to elude capture, evading them at every turn.

However, Briggs, feeling the weight of exhaustion settle upon him, slowed his pace. Christopher, fueled by youthful vigour and determination, surged forward, closing the gap between him and the figure. His steps were swift and agile, his focus unbroken as he relentlessly pursued her through the winding streets of the London ghetto.

The figure darted through alleyways and narrow passages, her movements seemingly effortless despite the fatigue that had undoubtedly begun to gnaw at her as well. She weaved through the labyrinthine streets, leaving a trail of chaos in her wake as she bumped into unsuspecting bystanders and collided with crates and barrels in her desperate bid to escape.

Undeterred by the obstacles, Christopher matched her every move with unwavering determination. He skillfully navigated through the maze-like alleys, jumping over obstacles and swiftly manoeuvring around corners as he closed the distance between them.

The dimly lit streets added an air of suspense to the chase, the mist clinging to the shadows as if conspiring with the morning fog to obscure their pursuit. The city's gritty atmosphere seemed to echo their relentless pursuit, heightening the tension as Christopher's footsteps echoed through the empty streets.

Finally, they reached a dead-end alley, the walls closing around them. The hooded figure stopped, her back pressed against the graffiti-covered brickwork. With nowhere left to run, she turned to face Christopher, her eyes filled with defiance and trepidation.

As the tension peaked in the dead-end corner, Christopher's exhaustion was momentarily overshadowed by a surge of adrenaline. He raised his weapon, pointing it directly at the woman with her back against him, his voice filled with urgency.

"Freeze! Don't make any sudden moves!"

The woman slowly turned around, revealing her face to Christopher. As their eyes met, a flicker of recognition and astonishment passed through his features. It was the same blue-eyed, dark-haired woman Elain had described earlier—Bretty Carter.

For a brief moment, Christopher found himself captivated by her beauty. The intensity momentarily faded into the background as he dropped his hands, his gaze fixed upon her. He couldn't help but be taken aback by the stark contrast between her striking appearance and the dangerous circumstances they found themselves in.

Aware of Christopher's stunned reaction, Brett raised an eyebrow and tilted her head slightly. A mixture of wariness and curiosity flashed across her face, uncertain how to interpret his unexpected response. She remained motionless, her hands slightly raised in a gesture of surrender.

Christopher's mind raced, attempting to reconcile the image of Bretty before him with the potential threat she may pose. He quickly refocused, reminding himself of their mission and the need for answers. Shaking off the momentary distraction, he regained his composure.

Regaining control of the situation, Christopher composed himself and spoke with a firmness that betrayed his initial surprise.

"Hands where I can see them, Bretty. We have questions that need answering. Don't make any sudden moves."

Brett, her expression shifting from curiosity to guarded determination, complied with Christopher's command. She slowly lowered her hands, her gaze locked with his.

Christopher gestured for Brett to step back from the corner without breaking eye contact, allowing a safe distance between them. The adrenaline coursing through his veins propelled him forward. His determination to unravel the mysteries surrounding their investigation reignited.

As the seconds ticked by, the resolute determination in Brett's eyes mirrored Christopher's own. Yet she had more defiance to it than his.

Briggs eventually came into the scene, catching up with Christopher. They stood side by side, facing Brett, who had her hands raised in surrender. The moment's intensity hung heavy in the air as they sought answers from her.

"What is your relationship with Tony Al Garfhr?" Briggs said, his voice firm and commanding, pressed Brett for information.

Bretty hesitated, her gaze flickering between the two detectives. The weight of the situation seemed to settle upon her, and the realization that her position was compromised became evident.

"He's my ex-boyfriend," Brett admitted, her voice tinged with bitterness and frustration. "He owes me a substantial amount of money. I moved into his place, hoping to confront him and get what he owes me."

Briggs' eyes narrowed, his grip tightening on his weapon as he processed the information.

"Why didn't you go to the authorities?" Briggs questioned, his voice laced with suspicion.

Brett's eyes darted from Briggs to Christopher and back again. She lowered her hands slowly, her gaze mixed with defiance and desperation. "I thought I could handle it on my own. I didn't trust the system to bring him to justice. I wanted to confront him and make him pay what he owed. Besides, Tony is a dangerous man. Inviting the police in on him is like calling death to come in on you."

Briggs exchanged a brief glance with Christopher. The lines between victim and suspect were beginning to blur, and they needed to tread carefully to uncover the truth.

"Where is Tony now?" Christopher interjected, his tone measured and intent on gathering crucial information.

Brett's eyes flickered, uncertainty crossing her features. "I don't know. He disappeared about a week ago. He went off the grid, and I haven't located him."

Briggs remained sceptical, his gaze unwavering. "You expect us to believe that? You were his girlfriend. You must know something."

A hint of desperation crept into Brett's voice as she responded, her eyes pleading for understanding. "I swear, I have no idea where he is. If I did, I wouldn't be standing before you. I wanted justice, not this."

'Why did you run when you saw us then' Briggs asked.

Bretty paused for a moment. 'Well, you're the cops. And I don't roll well with cops.'

'Who said we are cops? We don't have uniforms on?' Briggs said as he furrowed his eyebrow.

'I know one when I see one Bretty said

Silence settled upon the trio, the weight of their respective motivations and uncertainties hanging heavily in the air. The truth, like an elusive shadow, remained just beyond their reach.

The sun began to rise, casting its golden hues upon the dimly lit streets. The detectives and Brett stood at a crossroads. Briggs' gaze lingered on Brett, his eyes tracing the contours of her face, searching for clues to unravel the enigma she presented. There was an undeniable complexity within her, a juxtaposition of innocence and worldliness that seemed at odds with one another.

As he observed her, he couldn't help but feel a mix of sympathy and frustration. There was an air of vulnerability about her as if she had been thrust into a dangerous world beyond her control. It was a face that betrayed the weight of experiences far beyond her years, yet there was a lingering trace of youthfulness that hadn't been completely extinguished.

In Brett, Briggs saw the remnants of a young girl who had once possessed innocence, who may have been manipulated and taken advantage of by those with darker intentions. His mind drifted to Tony Al Garfhr, a man who seemed to relish in preying upon the vulnerabilities of young women like Brett.

He couldn't help but blame individuals like Tony, perverts who exploited and groomed innocent souls for their own gratification. The anger welled within him, deep-seated indignation against those who would strip away the purity and potential of others for their own twisted desires.

He realized that life had dealt her a difficult hand, thrusting her into a world where survival often required compromise and unsavoury choices. It was a harsh reality that forced her to dance with the devil, navigating treacherous waters with a delicate balance of self-preservation and resilience.

There was a weariness in Brett's eyes, a weariness that spoke of battles fought, scars earned, and hard-earned wisdom etched into her very being. It was as if she carried the world's weight upon her shoulders, burdened by experiences that had aged her beyond her years.

Briggs contemplated the paradox before him— the fragile strength and the tainted innocence. He couldn't help but wonder about the layers beneath her exterior, the untold stories, and the intricate web of circumstances that had brought her to this moment.

Yet, as Briggs continued to observe Brett, a flicker of scepticism mingled with his frustration. He couldn't trust her.

At that moment, the first rays of sunlight broke through the darkness. He couldn't shake the haunting image of Brett, a young girl who had danced with the devil, her face bearing the scars of a world that had chewed her up and spit her out.

Briggs tore his gaze away from Brett, his mind refocusing on the task. He knew deeper layers were to be uncovered, a truth that lay just beyond their grasp. With determination burning in his eyes, he stepped away from her, ready to navigate the treacherous path ahead.

He released his grip on his weapon, a momentary flicker of doubt crossing his face. He believed that Brett had nothing more to offer, that their encounter had been coincidental. He turned his back to leave the scene, his mind shifting gears to the next lead they could pursue.

Briggs felt Christopher's firm grip on his arm, preventing him from leaving the scene. 'We can't just leave her here, Briggs. Elain said she could lead us to where Tony is.'

The determination in Christopher's voice and mentioning Lainy's observations made Briggs pause. Reluctantly, Briggs turned back to face Brett, his expression a mix of curiosity and scepticism. Christopher's words sparked a glimmer of intrigue within him, urging him to reconsider. He glanced at Brett, studying her closely as she stood there, her hands still raised in surrender.

Christopher took a step closer, his tone earnest and persuasive. "Briggs, think about it. If Elain has witnessed Brett involved with these dangerous arms, she's likely been privy to Tony's interactions with these people. Elain mentioned seeing her involved with dangerous weaponry, which means she may have insights to help us piece together the puzzle."

Briggs contemplated Christopher's words, his mind churning with the possibilities. Clearly, Brett had information that could prove valuable to their investigation. Despite his initial doubts, he couldn't ignore the potential breakthrough that Brett's involvement could bring.

Briggs hesitated momentarily, his hand hovering over his weapon as Christopher's words echoed in his mind. Briggs turned to face Christopher, his brows furrowed in contemplation. He recognized the significance of what Christopher was proposing, the potential breakthrough that Brett could offer in their pursuit of justice.

With a sigh, Briggs conceded, his eyes never leaving Brett's. "Alright, Christopher, you've made your point. If Brett has witnessed Tony's interactions with these individuals, she could provide valuable insights and lead us closer to the truth."

As he spoke, Briggs glanced back at Brett, who stood before them with a mixture of apprehension and defiance. Her eyes darted between the two detectives, uncertainty etched on her face. He could sense her reluctance to cooperate, her general wariness.

Briggs turned back towards Brett, his gaze meeting hers. He saw a flicker of surprise and apprehension in her eyes as if she didn't expect him to reconsider. Slowly, he approached her, his demeanour cautious yet resolute.

"Brett," Briggs began, his voice measured, "Christopher has a point. We want to hear if you have any information that can lead us to Tony or shed light on the individuals responsible for these acts of violence."

Brett's expression wavered, torn between her own self-preservation and the weight of the secrets she carried. It was evident that trust did not come easily to her. She hesitated for a moment, her eyes darting between Briggs and Christopher.

Turning to Christopher, Briggs spoke with renewed determination. "Let's get back to the office and debrief. We have a lot to discuss and plan. This case just became even more complicated."

Briggs turned around to leave while Christopher swiftly retrieved a pair of handcuffs from his utility belt and approached Brett cautiously. He carefully secured the handcuffs around her wrists, ensuring she remained under their control. It was a necessary precaution, given the gravity of the situation and the potential risks involved.

Now restrained by the handcuffs, Brett cast a wary glance at Christopher, a mix of defiance and apprehension in her eyes.

Briggs and Christopher led Brett towards their waiting vehicle, their pace steady and purposeful. The streets still held an air of tension, as if they were walking through a city on the verge of awakening. The morning mist clung to the corners of the buildings, casting an eerie ambience that mirrored their mission's uncertainty.

Christopher opened the back door as they reached the car and motioned for Brett to enter. She hesitated momentarily, her eyes darting between the two detectives, searching for any signs of deceit or ill intent. But there was a determination etched on their faces, a resolve that resonated with her.

With a sigh, Brett climbed into the backseat, her hands restrained by the handcuffs. The cold metal pressed against her skin.

Briggs placed in the driver's seat, his grip firm on the steering wheel. Christopher settled in beside him, his focus unwavering as he kept a watchful eye on their captive. The engine roared to life, breaking the silence of the early morning.

As the vehicle moved through the dimly lit streets, the weight of the situation settled upon them. The road ahead was uncertain, fraught with challenges and dangers yet to be revealed. But they were united in their pursuit of justice, driven by a shared determination to unravel the truth and bring those responsible to account.

Brett sat in the backseat, her gaze fixed on the passing cityscape. Christopher watched her through the front mirror to determine what she was thinking. But he couldn't wrap his head around her thought. However, her face looked like a mixture of resignation, defiance and something dark Christopher was unfamiliar with.

With each passing mile, they drew closer to the heart of the truth. The city's shadows loomed around them, mirroring the shadows that had cast a veil of darkness over their lives. And as they ventured deeper into the unknown, they carried with them the weight of responsibility, the hope for justice, and the unspoken promise of redemption.

CHAPTER FOUR

Briggs stood in a dimly lit telephone booth, the walls covered in graffiti and the air thick with anticipation and apprehension. He took a deep breath, steeling himself for the conversation he knew he needed to have. Pulling out his phone, he dialled Racheal's number, the familiar tone ringing as he waited for her to pick up.

After a few rings, Racheal's voice came through the line, her tone laced with a hint of coldness. "Hello?" she answered curtly, her words lacking the usual warmth that Briggs had grown accustomed to.

Briggs cleared his throat, his voice tinged with remorse. "Hey, Racheal. It's me, Briggs. Look… I wanted to talk about what happened the day yesterday…. I'm sorry for the way things turned out. It wasn't what I had planned or expected."
There was a silence on the other end of the line,

'I'm just glad you were not hurt. I can't imagine what I'll do to myself if they ever hurt you.'

The silence remained, and soon it was followed by a sigh that carried a hint of frustration. "Apologies won't change what happened, Briggs," Racheal replied, her voice dripping with passive aggression. "This is not the first time you've put me in a dangerous situation, and I'm sick and tired of it. All I wanted was a fucking peaceful evening Briggs."

Briggs' heart sunk at the weight of Racheal's words. He had always strived to protect and shield her from the darkness that consumed his world, but it seemed he had failed again. "I understand how you feel, Racheal," he responded earnestly. "I never wanted to put you in harm's way. Look, you know how much you mean the world to me. I'll do whatever it takes to make it right. I promise you that."

There was a brief silence on the other end of the line. "Maybe it's best if we take a break," she said, her words hanging in the air with a heavyweight. , and Briggs could sense the turmoil in Racheal's voice as she spoke again. "I need some time to think and figure things out."

That moment Briggs felt a lump form in his throat, his mind racing to comprehend what Racheal was suggesting. "A break?" he asked, his voice filled with confusion and desperation. "You don't mean...a breakup, do you?"

Before he could get a response, the line went dead. Racheal hung up. The abruptness of the disconnection left Briggs alone in the cramped telephone booth. A wave of emotions washed over him. He leaned against the booth's graffiti-covered wall, trying to gather his thoughts amidst the chaos that had suddenly engulfed his world.

With a heavy sigh, Briggs knew deep down that Racheal was right and had to respect Racheal's request for space. He realised that his actions had consequences, and he couldn't expect her to continue enduring the dangers of being a part of his life. The weight of his decisions settled upon him, a burden he carried as he stepped out of the telephone booth and into the bustling city street.

Briggs stepped out of the phone booth, the weight of his conversation with Racheal still lingering in his mind. He emerged onto the bustling city street and spotted Christopher waiting for him, leaning casually against a nearby lamppost. Their eyes met, and a silent understanding passed between them without exchanging words.

Christopher gave Briggs a knowing nod, conveying they both knew what to do. Together, they made their way through the busy streets, their footsteps falling in sync as they navigated through the hustle and bustle of the city. Their destination was a nondescript warehouse tucked away from prying eyes, a place where secrets were whispered and truths were uncovered.

As they reached the warehouse entrance, Briggs pushed open the heavy metal door, revealing a dimly lit interior. The air inside was filled with the scent of must and anticipation, a tangible reminder of the mysteries waiting to be unravelled within those walls.

They stepped into the warehouse, their footsteps echoing against the cold concrete floor. Shelves lined with boxes and crates towered above them, casting long shadows in the dim light. It was a place that held secrets, a sanctuary for their investigations.

Christopher took the lead, his keen eyes scanning the surroundings, always alert to the slightest hint of danger. While Briggs followed closely behind.

As they ventured deeper into the warehouse, they passed rows upon rows of stacked boxes, each holding a story waiting to be discovered.

Soon Briggs and Christopher settled into a space within the warehouse and their attention was drawn to a figure bound to a chair in the corner of the room. It was Bretty, the enigmatic woman they had pursued earlier. She was tightly restrained, her wrists and ankles securely bound with ropes. A strip of duct tape covered her lips, preventing her from speaking or making any sound.

Bretty's eyes darted around the room. Her attempts to communicate through frantic movements met with resistance from the restraints. The determination in her gaze was palpable, her silent pleas for freedom evident even without words. It was clear that she wanted to convey something of great importance.

Christopher, observing the scene, turned to Briggs and spoke in a low voice, ensuring their conversation remained private within the confines of the warehouse. "I made sure she wouldn't escape," he informed Briggs, his tone firm and confident. "She won't be able to loosen those restraints easily."

Briggs nodded, acknowledging Christopher's assurance. He understood the necessity of keeping Bretty securely bound, as her potential knowledge about Tony Al Garfhr and the sources of the harms they were investigating made her a valuable piece in their puzzle. There was a complexity to her that he couldn't quite grasp, and he wondered if she held the key to unravelling the truth.

Approaching Bretty cautiously, Briggs looked into her eyes, his gaze filled with curiosity and concern. He reached for the strip of duct tape covering her mouth, slowly peeling it away to grant her the ability to speak. As the tape came off, Bretty's lips moved, forming words that had been restrained for too long.

"Let me go!" Bretty imploded, her voice tinged with desperation. "I've told you what you wanted to know. Let me go!"

Briggs paused for a moment, considering her plea. But she sounded like a failed actress, and Briggs could see right through it.

"I understand your desire to be free, Bretty," Briggs responded, his voice firm. "But you possess information that is vital to our investigation. Tony Al Garfhr is dangerous, and we must bring him to justice before he causes any more harm."

Bretty's expression shifted, a mix of defiance and amusement playing across her face. She let out a cynical chuckle, her smirk revealing a glimpse of the darkness that seemed to dwell within her. "You think we have the same enemy, don't you?" she asked, her voice laced with a hint of irony. "Well, you might be right. I'd be more than glad to track Tony down and end him."

Briggs studied Bretty's face, searching for any signs of deception. He could sense her thirst for revenge, the burning desire to make Tony pay for the pain he had caused her. It was a dangerous motivation, but one that aligned with their mission. If Bretty had the knowledge and the determination to help them dismantle the web of harm Tony had spun, perhaps it was worth the risk.

"I won't release you just yet, Bretty," Briggs said, his voice resolute. "But I'll consider your offer. In the meantime, you must tell us everything you know about Tony—his associates, activities, anything that can help us bring him down."

Bretty nodded, her eyes glinting with a newfound sense of purpose. She seems to understand that her freedom hinged upon her cooperation and ability to contribute to their cause.

"I started dating Tony about two years ago," Bretty revealed, her voice tinged with bitterness. "He promised me the world, said he would marry me. I believed him, but little did I know he was nothing more than a promiscuous jerk with a string of baby mamas."

A sense of disappointment resonated in Bretty's voice as she recalled the shattered dreams and broken promises. She had fallen for Tony's charm, only to discover his true nature.

This was believable to Briggs who knew Tony very well. His honeycomb tongue wasn't just for swaying women but men alike. He could sway the toughest man in the room, who lets his guard down about who Tony is, and make him do his selfish bidding.

Bretty continued 'It was the moment I moved in with him that my eyes were truly opened to the dangerous activities he was involved in.' Bretty said and stopped to catch her breath.

"It was when I moved in with Tony that I saw the other side of him," Bretty continued, her voice filled with fear and determination. "He was knee-deep in illegal dealings, connections with shady characters, and dangerous operations. I witnessed things I never thought possible."

Bretty's revelations painted a picture of a man deeply entangled in criminal activities. Her eyes scanned the room as if reliving the memories, her hands fidgeting with the restraints that held her captive. The unease in the air was palpable, a testament to the dangerous world they found themselves in.

But amidst the darkness, Bretty had also acquired skills necessary for their mission. Tony had trained her to handle firearms, knowing the importance of self-defence in their perilous journey.

"He taught me how to handle a gun," Bretty admitted, her voice filled with bitterness and gratitude. "He wanted me to be able to defend ourselves, to survive during the chaos he had created."

Briggs and Christopher listened intently, focusing solely on Bretty's every word.

Briggs contemplated this newfound revelation again. It was very plausible. Bretty's story painted a vivid image of a woman who had been deceived, used as a pawn in Tony's dangerous game. Her journey from naivety to awareness mirrored their own, and Briggs couldn't help but feel a sense of empathy for the woman who had found herself entangled in the same web of darkness.

Briggs paced back and forth, his impatience growing as he considered the next move in their investigation. The weight of the situation bore heavily on his shoulders, and he felt the urgency to uncover the truth. He paused abruptly, a determined look in his eyes, and reached into the inner pocket of his jacket.

Withdrawing a folded piece of paper, that was yellow in colour, Briggs unfolded it carefully. The paper bore a distinctive sign, its bold presence demanding attention. Intricate hieroglyphics and coded symbols adorned its surface, representing a complex language only decipherable to those initiated in espionage.

He held the paper before Bretty, his gaze fixed on her intently. "Have you ever seen Tony associated with anything like this?" Briggs inquired, his voice firm yet tinged with a glimmer of hope. The question's weight hung in the air, as they both understood the potential significance of her response.

Bretty's eyes narrowed as she studied the cryptic symbols on the paper. The room fell into a contemplative silence, broken only by the soft sounds of her restrained breath. After a brief pause, she nodded slowly, her expression thoughtful.

"Yes," Bretty finally spoke, her voice filled with uncertainty and recognition. "I've seen Tony with similar markings before. He had a hidden compartment in his office where he kept documents with similar codes."

Briggs' heart skipped a beat, adrenaline coursing through his veins. The paper in his hand suddenly held an even greater significance. It confirmed their suspicions and opened a new avenue of investigation, leading them closer to unravelling the intricate web of secrets.

"Tell me everything you know," Briggs demanded, steady but laced with anticipation. "Every detail, every encounter, no matter how insignificant it may seem."

Bretty complied, her words flowing with a newfound determination. She recounted instances where she had glimpsed Tony working with encoded documents, exchanging information with unknown associates, and engaging in clandestine meetings. With each revelation, the pieces of the puzzle began to fit together, forming a clearer picture of the sinister world Tony inhabited.

'...there was this time Tony delivered a set of weapons to Durango. I remember spotting Durango and his men with these tattoos on their left arm...these symbols were even on their shirts.

Bretty's revelation sent a shiver down Briggs' spine. The name "Durango" carried a notorious reputation in the underworld, and his association with Tony raised the stakes of their investigation to a whole new level. The fact that Durango and his men bore the same symbols as the ones on the paper heightened the significance of their connection.

Briggs leaned in closer, his eyes fixed on Bretty. "Tell me everything you know about Durango and his operation," he urged, his voice filled with urgency and determination.

Bretty took a deep breath, her eyes reflecting the gravity of the situation. "Tony mentioned that

Durango was a highly dangerous individual, involved in arms smuggling and other illicit activities," she began. "He operates from a hidden base on the city's outskirts, where he keeps a tight-knit group of loyal followers. They are known for ruthlessness and adherence to a strict code of secrecy. It's like a cult"

She continued, detailing Tony's interactions with Durango and the tasks he had assigned her in their collaboration. Bretty had been unwittingly drawn into a world of darkness, compelled to fulfil Tony's orders without truly comprehending the consequences.

Briggs listened intently, absorbing every detail, as he began to formulate a plan in his mind. It was clear that Durango held valuable information, and their encounter with Bretty might provide the key to infiltrating his operation and dismantling the terrorist network.

"Thank you, Bretty," Briggs said, his voice filled with gratitude. Yet he looked deep in contemplation. "Your cooperation is invaluable...'

he said absentmindedly as he tried to comb through the information Bretty had just given him.

Briggs turned to Christopher, he said without matching his eyes, as he was still deep in contemplation. "We need to gather more intelligence on Durango and his operation. We must uncover his base, infiltrate his ranks, and neutralise the threat he poses."

Christopher nodded, wondering what was on Briggs's mind. The mission had become more intricate and dangerous, but they were resolute in pursuing justice. Since he had been appointed to work with Briggs, Briggs had never ceased to be an intelligent yet enigmatic fellow. Briggs had his own way of figuring deep things out in his mind while he keeps everyone away with their breath held looking up to him for answers, interpretation or the next move to take.

Briggs turned away from Bretty and walked a little distance from the scene. His mind raced with a flurry of thoughts and memories. The puzzle pieces were finally beginning to fall into place, and a chilling realisation washed over him. The symbol that Bretty was recognized on the paper and associated with Durango was the same symbol he had seen on the arms of the men he had apprehended yesterday with Racheal at their dinner.

Adrenaline coursed through Briggs' veins as he made the connection. It couldn't be a mere coincidence. Durango's symbol on those men indicated they were a part of his criminal network.

A wave of determination swept over Briggs as he began to piece together the implications of this revelation. If Durango's men were involved in trying to assassinate him. There is a huge probability they were the ones involved in the assassination of the FBI agents and their families and the subsequent attacks, it meant that they were working under Durango's orders.

He had heard of Durango several times but had not gotten enough time to dig up the extent of his activities and the danger he posed. The piece of information he knows about Durango didn't reveal him to be a deeply entrenched and arsenated warlord who would go after the state. Durango didn't seem like someone with the balls to go after the state.

That moment Briggs felt a mix of frustration and determination wash over him as he contemplated the latest turn of events. He had hoped that the evidence they had gathered at Thomas' basement would be the key to cracking the case wide open. However, the recent revelations had shown that their journey was far from over. They seemed to be met with more complexities and unanswered questions with every step forward.

Rubbing his head in frustration, Briggs couldn't help but feel a sense of discouragement creeping in. The case had become a tangled web of deceit, with Tony's involvement reaching deeper than they had initially anticipated. The connections to Durango and his criminal network added another layer of complexity to an already convoluted investigation.

But amidst the frustration, Briggs felt a flicker of determination ignite. He had dedicated his life to upholding justice and protecting innocent lives, and he wasn't about to let a few setbacks deter him. If anything, the recent evidence and revelations only reinforced his resolve.

As Briggs pondered the situation, a nagging feeling of unease settled within him. It didn't add up that Tony would simply run away, leaving behind his weapons and power over others. He knew Tony all too well, understanding the manipulative nature of the man and his ability to talk his way out of almost any predicament.

In Briggs' experience, when Briggs come around to interrogate him, Tony would have employed his silver tongue to attempt to negotiate his way out of trouble. He would have denied involvement in the crimes they were investigating, even though both Briggs and Tony were fully aware of his guilt. Tony would have likely offered a drink, a seemingly friendly gesture to establish a false camaraderie, only to passively threaten Briggs to stay off his trail.

It was a familiar dance where Tony would play the part of the smug, elusive villain, toying with Briggs as he teased information, always dangling it just out of reach. The routine would involve a high-stakes negotiation, with Tony demanding a hefty sum in exchange for revealing crucial details. It was a game they had played before, a twisted form of cat and mouse.

But now, Tony had vanished without a trace. Something didn't feel right to Briggs, and he didn't like it one bit. It was as if Tony had deviated from his well-established modus operandi, leaving behind a void of uncertainty. It unsettled Briggs, stirring a mix of frustration and curiosity within him.

Briggs understood that there was more to this puzzle than he initially thought. Tony's sudden disappearance indicated a significant shift in the dynamics of their investigation. It raised questions about their danger and the true scope of Tony's criminal activities.

Deep in thought, Briggs resolved to uncover the truth. He knew that to get to the bottom of this, he would have to dig deeper, follow every lead, and scrutinise every piece of evidence. Tony's disappearance was a puzzle piece they couldn't afford to ignore, and it held the potential to unlock a deeper layer of deception and danger.

As he contemplated his next move, Briggs turned to Bretty. He walked purposefully back towards Bretty, his expression resolute. He untied her and asked her to leave. He could see the confusion in her eyes, wondering why he would suddenly let her go when she expressed willingness to join their mission.

"Bretty," Briggs started, his voice firm. "I appreciate your willingness to help. I won't risk your safety any longer. This mission has taken an unexpected turn, becoming more dangerous by the minute. I need you to leave, to stay away from this."

Bretty looked at Briggs, a mixture of confusion and frustration evident on her face. She opened her mouth to protest, but Briggs raised his hand, cutting her off.

"I understand that you want to be a part of this, that you want to help bring Tony down," Briggs continued, his tone still firm. "But right now, it's best if you keep your distance from these people"

Bretty's eyes darted between Briggs and Christopher, uncertainty and determination warring within her. She didn't look pleased with Briggs with conclusion.

Christopher, observing the exchange, looked hesitant to leave Bretty behind. He knew the risks and importance of her insights and assistance in their mission. He stepped forward, his expression a mix of concern and determination.

"Briggs, are you sure about this?" Christopher asked, his voice reflecting his reluctance. "We could use her help. She knows more about Tony and Durango than anyone else."

Briggs sighed, his gaze shifting between Christopher and Bretty. He understood Christopher's perspective but couldn't ignore the nagging feeling that getting Bretty involved was a bad idea.

"We can't take the risk," Briggs replied, his voice steady. "I need you to trust me on this. I'll keep Bretty informed, and if there's an opportunity for her to assist us safely in the future, we'll consider it. But for now, she must be out of harm's way."

Christopher hesitated for a moment, his gaze lingering on Bretty. Finally, he nodded, his trust in Briggs overriding his reservations. He turned to Bretty and then back to Briggs who had started heading out of the warehouse.

As they approached the door, preparing to leave, Bretty's sudden outburst caught Briggs and Christopher off guard.

'I know where Durango is! I could help you find him.'

They paused in their steps, exchanging surprised glances. Bretty's voice echoed with determination.

Christopher swiftly turned around, his eyes lighting up with hope and intrigue. He knew the importance of Durango's role in the investigation and recognized that Bretty's knowledge could prove invaluable. He stepped closer to her, ready to delve deeper into the details she possessed.

Briggs, however, remained hesitant. He felt a pang of caution, his mind flooded with questions. Why would Durango want him dead? What connection did he have to this dangerous criminal? He couldn't ignore the foreboding that tugged at him, urging him to proceed cautiously.

After a brief pause, Briggs turned slowly, his gaze fixed on Bretty. He studied her carefully. But all he saw this time was a fiery determination in her eyes, a genuine desire to bring Tony down and seek justice.

"Tell us everything you know about Durango," Briggs said, his voice a mix of caution and resolve. "If there's a chance to bring Tony down and stop the violence he's been orchestrating, we can't afford to ignore it. But remember, Bretty, trust is a two-way street. We need the whole truth."

Bretty nodded, her expression resolute. She proceeded to share what she knew about Durango, his secret base, and the inner workings of his criminal network. It became clear that Durango held a personal vendetta against Briggs, though the exact reasons remained elusive.

As Bretty continued speaking, Briggs couldn't help but feel sceptical about her claims. He crossed his arms and leaned against a nearby crate, his expression showing disbelief. To him, Bretty seemed like an inexperienced individual who may have been caught up in Tony's web of deceit.

Her words sounded too good to be true, and he couldn't help but wonder if she was exaggerating or making up stories to gain their trust. Briggs had seen his fair share of manipulative individuals in his work, and he knew better than to trust someone based solely on their words.

He glanced at Christopher, who seemed torn between curiosity and caution. Christopher's eyes conveyed his willingness to give Bretty a chance, but Briggs held his reservations.

"Look, Bretty," Briggs interjected, his voice laced with scepticism. "I appreciate your willingness to help and your claims about knowing Durango. But forgive me if I find it hard to believe everything you say. We need solid evidence and reliable leads to track down Tony and end this. I can't just rely on someone's word alone."

Bretty's face fell slightly, disappointment evident in her eyes. "I understand your concerns, Briggs," Bretty replied, her voice tinged with determination. "But I have seen things. I know places Tony frequents, and I can lead you to

Durango. I want to make things right and ensure justice is served. Just give me a chance. Please"

Briggs felt his phone vibrate in his pocket, and he pulled it out to see an incoming call from Alexander Q, his superior. He furrowed his brow, wondering what urgent matter required his attention. With a sigh, he answered the call and listened intently to what Alexander had to say.

As Alexander spoke on the other end, his tone serious and sombre, Briggs's expression grew solemn. He nodded in understanding, not uttering a single word throughout the conversation. After a brief exchange, Briggs ended the call, his mind now occupied with the weight of the news he had just received.

He turned to Christopher, his face etched with determination. 'We need to prepare for a funeral. The fallen FBI agents and their families would be laid to rest today. We are to pay their respects an honour their sacrifice.

Christopher nodded in understanding, his own expression mirroring Briggs's determined look. Briggs took the lead, heading out of the warehouse. He couldn't shake off the gravity of the situation, knowing that they had lost colleagues and innocent lives in their pursuit of justice. As they drove towards the location of the funeral, the atmosphere inside the vehicle was heavy with sorrow and determination.

Briggs and Christopher arrived at the cemetery in their inconspicuous black car, blending in with the sea of mourners dressed in sombre attire. The air was heavy with grief as they navigated through the crowded grounds. Briggs turned to Christopher, his voice low but firm, emphasizing the need for vigilance.

"Stay alert, Christopher," Briggs cautioned, his eyes scanning the surroundings through the car's window for any signs of potential threats. "We can't rule out the possibility that these psychopaths might try to exploit the vulnerability of this gathering. Keep your eyes peeled."

In unison, they reached for their concealed weapons, drawing them out and discreetly tucking them into their dark suits. The weight of the firearms bore into their suit, and they carefully clad it with their hands

Stepping out of the car, they seamlessly merged into the crowd, their presence blending with the sea of mourners paying their respects. The cemetery was filled with hushed conversations, the occasional sniffle, and the solemn silence that enveloped the atmosphere.

As they approached the designated area where the funeral service would occur, their focus remained unwavering. They maintained a subtle but effective presence, their training allowing them to blend in effortlessly while maintaining a keen awareness of their surroundings.

The sight of grieving families and friends, their faces etched with sorrow, reinforced the gravity of the situation. Briggs felt a pang of empathy for those who had lost their loved ones, and a renewed determination to bring justice to those responsible for such senseless tragedies.

The cemetery sprawled before them, an expanse of rolling hills adorned with rows of white marble tombstones. The sky hung heavy and pregnant with moisture, casting a sombre and melancholic mood over the scene. Briggs and Christopher stepped further into the scene, they were met with the sight of eleven caskets lined up side by side, each adorned with photographs of the fallen.

The photographs depicted not just the men who had lost their lives, but also their wives and children, a painful reminder of the families left behind to grieve. The images captured moments of joy and togetherness, frozen in time, now serving as a testament to the void left by their absence. It was a heartbreaking sight that tugged at the depths of one's emotions.

Mourners dressed in black filled the cemetery, their faces etched with sorrow and tears streaming down their cheeks. The atmosphere was heavy with grief, the silence broken only by hushed conversations and intermittent sobs. The collective weight of the loss was palpable, as the mourners sought solace in one another's presence, finding strength in shared pain.

As Briggs and Christopher made their way towards the gathering, the grass beneath their feet felt soft and damp, and a reflection of the impending rain. The scent of wet earth mingled with the sea of floral tributes, adding a bittersweet fragrance to the air. Dark clouds loomed overhead, casting a gloomy hue over the entire scene, as if the sky wept for the fallen.

The rows of white tombstones stretched out into the distance, a silent reminder of the countless lives laid to rest in this sacred ground. Each tombstone, meticulously carved and polished, stood as a solemn tribute to those who had passed on. Some were adorned with fresh flowers and mementoes, evidence of the ongoing remembrance and love bestowed upon the departed.

The wind whispered through the trees, rustling leaves and adding a mournful melody. The occasional roll of thunder reverberated through the atmosphere, heightening the sense of anticipation and sorrow. It seemed as though even nature mourned the loss of these brave souls, preparing to unleash a heavy downpour as if to mirror the tears shed by those gathered.

Briggs and Christopher joined the mourners, their dark suits blending seamlessly with the sea of black attire. Their solemn expressions mirrored the gravity of the occasion, their hearts heavy with respect and determination. They stood side by side, paying their respects to the fallen, their heads bowed quickly in silent contemplation.

Around them, loved ones embraced, seeking solace in the shared sorrow. Tears flowed freely, expressions of grief mingling with memories of happier times. The weight of loss hung heavy in the air, a palpable reminder of the sacrifices made to pursue justice.

As the ceremony commenced, the sombre tones of prayers and eulogies filled the air. The officiant's words echoed through the cemetery, offering comfort and hope amidst the sea of sorrow. The mourners, united in their grief, clung to each word, finding solace in the collective embrace of the community.

The air was still, and anticipation loomed, heightening the emotional intensity. Dark clouds continued to gather above, casting a shadow over the mourners. The atmosphere was pregnant with unshed tears, as if nature held its breath, waiting for release.

As the ceremony began, the officiant's voice resonated through the cemetery, offering words of comfort and solace. The air grew heavy with emotion as eulogies were spoken, each one a tribute to the lives lost and the impact they had made. Tears flowed freely, expressions of grief mingling with memories of cherished moments.

The absence of raindrops, for now, added a sense of suspended time. The threatening clouds loomed overhead, casting a grey hue over the scene. Though the rain had yet to fall, the atmosphere crackled with a quiet intensity, as if nature held its breath.

Briggs and Christopher moved through the cemetery with purpose, their eyes constantly scanning the surroundings, alert for any suspicious behaviour or signs of danger. They knew that in a gathering of this magnitude, where emotions ran high, and vulnerabilities were exposed, there was a heightened risk of being targeted.

Briggs and Christopher, their eyes shielded behind dark sunglasses, stood tall and vigilant amidst the sea of mourners dressed in black. The sunglasses were a barrier, concealing their thoughts and emotions from prying eyes. They surveyed their surroundings with stoic expressions, their keen senses attuned to any sign of potential danger.

The mourners, draped in mourning attire, moved slowly and with a sombre air. Faces etched with grief, their eyes downcast, they paid their respects to the fallen agents. The atmosphere was heavy with sorrow, and a hushed silence enveloped the cemetery, broken only by the occasional sob or whispered condolence.

Briggs and Christopher's sharp eyes scanned the crowd, their gaze shifting from one figure to another. Every movement and gesture was assessed, their instincts honed by years of training and experience. They knew that even in this solemn moment, danger could lurk in the shadows, waiting to strike.

As they observed the mourners, their eyes caught fleeting glances of suspicion and curiosity. Some faces seemed familiar, their features reminiscent of those they had encountered during their investigations. The possibility that Durango's men could be among the mourners heightened their vigilance.

But amidst the crowd of mourners, grief etched on their faces, it was challenging to discern friend from foe. Each person appeared immersed in their private sorrow, seeking solace and closure for their personal loss. The collective grief formed a shield that guarded secrets and intentions, making it difficult for Briggs and Christopher to identify potential threats.

The sunglasses shielded their eyes, allowing them to observe discreetly without betraying their intentions. Behind the dark lenses, their gaze darted from face to face, searching for any sign of familiarity, any hint of malicious intent.

Briggs and Christopher maintained a respectful distance as they moved through the crowd, careful not to disrupt the mourning process. They communicated silently, exchanging subtle nods and gestures to convey their observations and share any potential concerns.

At that moment, Briggs felt a nagging intuition gnawing at his gut, warning him something was amiss. The request from Alexander Q to attend the funeral had stirred his suspicions, suggesting that there might be more to this gathering than just mourning the fallen agents. He discreetly signalled to Christopher, silently communicating the need to split up and investigate separately.

With a subtle nod, Christopher acknowledged Briggs' signal, understanding the urgency and the importance of gathering more information. They discreetly moved away from each other, their dark suits blending seamlessly into the sea of mourners.

Briggs carefully weaved through the crowd, his senses on high alert. He observed the subtle shifts in body language, the whispered conversations, and the darting glances exchanged between individuals. The atmosphere crackled with an undercurrent of tension, further fuelling his unease.

As he moved amidst the mourners, Briggs noticed a small group huddled together in intense conversation. Their gestures were animated, their eyes darting around as if assessing their surroundings. Intrigued, Briggs quietly edged closer, careful not to attract attention.

From a distance, he overheard snippets of their conversation, catching phrases like "unresolved matters," "unfinished business," and "it's time to act." His heart rate quickened, and adrenaline coursed through his veins. These were not typical mourning conversations; they held a sense of urgency and purpose that struck him as suspicious.

In such situations, Briggs discreetly reached into his pocket and retrieved a small device, his secret weapon. It was a high-tech audio surveillance device that allowed him to eavesdrop safely. He discreetly activated the device and concealed it within the palm of his hand, positioning himself strategically to capture their conversation.

Christopher was momentarily drawn to the sea of flowers adorning the gravesites as he scanned the scene. Among the myriad colours and varieties, one type stood out to him—the white lotus flowers. They were scattered throughout the cemetery, their delicate petals and elegant stems creating a serene and ethereal atmosphere.

White lotus flowers held a special significance for Christopher. They were his late mother's favourite flowers, which she had always admired and cherished. The sight of them brought back memories of her, her gentle smile, and her unwavering love.

He recalled the day of her burial, when the entire ceremony was adorned with white lotus flowers. The fragrance permeated the air, mingling with the collective grief and offering a sense of tranquillity and solace amidst the heartache.

White lotus flowers at the current funeral stirred emotions within Christopher. It reminded him of the loss he had experienced in his own life, amplifying the weight of grief that hung heavy in the air. Yet, amidst the sorrow, there was also a sense of comfort, knowing that his mother's favourite flowers were present. She told him the white lotus symbolised purity, beauty, and rebirth.

The white lotus flowers seemed to be intentionally scattered, as if carefully placed by loving hands to pay homage to the fallen agents. Christopher was captivated by their delicate petals, their pure white colour contrasting against the dark attire of the mourners.

The significance of the white lotus flowers was not lost on Christopher. They served as a reminder of life's cyclical nature, the fragility of existence, and the need to find strength and resilience in the face of adversity. It was a subtle reminder to carry on the legacy of those who had been lost. To honour the memory of his mother by pursuing justice and truth.

With a renewed sense of purpose, Christopher ignored the flowers and focused on his surroundings. The mystery surrounding Durango and the potential threat lurking amid the mourners again took precedence.

Christopher's gaze shifted from the sea of mourners to a little girl standing in the distance, holding a single red lotus flower. Her presence amidst the solemn atmosphere caught his attention, and he felt compelled to approach her.

Curious, he approached the girl, his steps measured and deliberate.

As he drew closer, Christopher noticed the girl's cherubic face, framed by a black beret that added a touch of innocence and charm to her appearance. Her bright blue eyes sparkled with a hint of mischief, and a faint blush adorned her cheeks as she realized Christopher's approach.

"Hello there," Christopher greeted her with a warm smile, trying to put her at ease. "That's a pretty red lotus you've got there. May I ask why you chose red instead of white?"

The little girl's eyes widened in surprise, perhaps unaccustomed to an adult taking an interest in her flower choice. She hesitated momentarily, shyness and excitement evident in her demeanour. With a gentle nod, she pointed towards a spot nearby, indicating someone or something.

Curiosity piqued, Christopher followed her gaze, his eyes scanning the area she had pointed to.

However, to his surprise, he found no one there, just an empty space that seemed inconspicuous and unremarkable. He furrowed his brow, a slight sense of bewilderment washing over him.

Confused, Christopher turned his attention back to the little girl, a mix of intrigue and concern in his voice. "I'm sorry, but I don't see anyone there. Who were you pointing to?"

The girl's blush deepened, and she fidgeted with the hem of her dress, seemingly uncertain about how to articulate her response. After a brief moment, she spoke in a soft, innocent voice, barely above a whisper.

"He's my secret friend," she murmured, her voice filled with a childlike wonder. "He told me that red lotus flowers bring luck and protection, so I picked it. But he's shy and doesn't want to come out."

Christopher's interest was piqued by the girl's words. Could it be that she was referring to an imaginary friend? Or perhaps there was something more mysterious at play?

Leaning slightly to be on eye level with the girl, Christopher asked gently, "What does your secret friend look like? Is he here with us now?"

The girl's eyes twinkled mischievously, a playful smile tugging at the corners of her lips.

Christopher's gaze shifted towards the flower the little girl clutched tightly to her chest, his eyes widened in recognition. There, a familiar symbol was tapped to the delicate petals of the red lotus—a hieroglyphic-like code that he had encountered during their investigation. His heart skipped a beat as he tried to get a clearer look at the symbol, sensing its potential significance.

Instinctively, Christopher reached out towards the flower, his fingers gently attempting to pry it from the girl's grasp. However, to his surprise, the little girl resisted, her grip tightening around the stem as she pulled it closer to her chest.

"No, you can't have it," the girl protested, her voice filled with determination and protectiveness. "My friend asked me not to let anyone have it. It's a special flower, and I must lay it down for Johnny."

Christopher's brows furrowed as he listened to her words. It became clear to him that the girl held a deeper connection to the fallen agents' family than he had initially realized. Perhaps one of their sons. The flower was a personal tribute, a way for her to honour and remember her friend, one of the children who had died in the tragic incident.

Realization washed over Christopher, the little girl standing before him was likely a close friend or classmate of the deceased child, harbouring her grief and sorrow. From her innocent perspective, she had formed a bond with her friend's memory and was determined to carry out this small act of remembrance.

A profound sense of empathy flooded Christopher's heart. With a tender smile,

Christopher withdrew his hand, respecting the girl's wishes.

"I understand, little one," he said softly, his voice gentle and understanding. "That flower is special to you, and honouring your friend is important. Take your time and find the perfect place to lay it down. I'm sure your friend will appreciate the gesture."

The girl's eyes shimmered with gratitude and relief, as if acknowledging the understanding she had found in Christopher's words. She nodded earnestly, her trust in him evident, and clutched the red lotus closer to her heart.

A sudden rumble echoed through the sky as Christopher squatted before the little girl, signalling a storm's imminent arrival. The deep, resonant sound of thunder reverberated across the cemetery, underscoring the weight of the gathering clouds. The atmosphere grew heavy, as if pregnant with anticipation, and the once bright cement paths darkened under the shadow of the approaching tempest.

Dark, brooding clouds loomed overhead, painting the sky in shades of grey and charcoal. The air crackled with an electric energy, intensifying the sense of impending rainfall. It seemed like nature held its breath, preparing to release the deluge building within the pregnant sky.

Yet, despite the ominous signs and the thunderous warning, the rain remained withheld. The atmosphere grew increasingly charged, creating an eerie stillness that enveloped the cemetery. Time seemed to stretch, as if caught in a suspended moment, awaiting the release of the impending storm.

Christopher glanced upwards, his gaze drawn to the swirling clouds obscuring the once-blue expanse. He felt a peculiar tension in the air, a palpable anticipation that matched the turmoil within his own being. It was as if the heavens mirrored the uncertainty and unease over their investigation.

The distant roll of thunder served as a reminder of the forces at play, the clash between light and darkness, justice and corruption. The impending storm symbolized the turbulent journey ahead, the challenges they would face in pursuing truth and justice for the fallen agents.

Christopher returned to the spot the little girl had pointed to again. This time his heart skipped a beat. Standing there now was a man, his presence exuding an aura of darkness and malevolence. The man's sinister smile sent a shiver down Christopher's spine, evoking a sense of foreboding and danger.

The stranger's eyes locked onto Christopher's, holding an intensity that seemed to penetrate his soul. The smile on his face hinted at a twisted pleasure derived from their unexpected encounter. In the man's hand, he held his wristwatch, a seemingly innocuous object that now held a sense of ominous significance.

With deliberate and deliberate movement, the man raised his wristwatch high in the air, its glimmering surface catching the limited light that pierced through the thick canopy of clouds. He tapped the watch lightly with his finger. The dark smile etched on the man's face deepened, accentuating the malevolent energy surrounding him.

At that moment something clicked in Christopher's mind. He looked at the flower the little girl held closely to her chest and the man and then from the man to the flower. Within the flower was a slow and quiet beeping with a soft glow blinking red light that penetrated its petals.

In that split second of realization, Christopher's senses heightened and his instincts kicked into overdrive. Without hesitation, he lunged forward, snatching the flower from the little girl's grasp. His muscles tensed, his heart pounding in his chest, as he swiftly propelled the flower through the air towards the open casket resting on the ground.

Time seemed to slow down as the flower soared through the air, its trajectory aligning with the casket. With a resounding thud, the flower made contact, its delicate form landing gracefully amidst the sombre setting. But just as it landed, an intense explosion shattered the air, a detonation that sent shockwaves rippling outward, engulfing everyone in its path.

The blast reverberated through the cemetery, a forceful wave swept across the ground. Mourners were caught off guard, their bodies jolted backward as the shockwave cascaded through the air. A chorus of screams and cries filled the space, mingling with the dissonant echoes of chaos and confusion.

Christopher, caught in the blast's radius, was thrown off balance, his body propelled backwards by the sheer force of the explosion. The ground rushed up to meet him, as if time itself had been disrupted by this unforeseen catastrophe. Dust and debris filled the air, creating an obscuring haze further intensifying the disorienting scene.

As the dust began to settle, Christopher, his senses still reeling, struggled to regain his composure. He could hear the sound of moans and groans, mingling with the cacophony of chaos. His vision blurred momentarily, but his determination remained unyielding.

Blinking away the remnants of dust that clung to his lashes, Christopher surveyed the explosion's aftermath. Once pristine and solemn, the casket lay shattered, its fragments scattered across the ground like broken dreams. The flower that had triggered this catastrophic event had been transformed into a weapon, its innocent guise concealing a deadly payload.

At that moment chaos erupted in the cemetery, as the peaceful atmosphere was shattered by the cacophony of gunfire and whizzing bullets, Christopher's instincts kicked into high gear. With a quick glance towards the little girl, he found solace in seeing her unharmed.

Her mother frantically screaming, ' Lola!' ran towards her and embraced her tightly. She picked her up and ran off with the other mourners trying to escape the scene. Assured of her safety,

Christopher turned his attention to the unfolding mayhem.

Drawing his gun from its holster, Christopher scanned the tumultuous scene, his eyes darting from one potential threat to another. The once solemn gathering now resembled a battlefield, with mourners scrambling for cover and cries of panic intermingling with the continuous bursts of gunfire.

In the distance, he spotted the figure of the sinister man who had taunted him moments before. The man seemed to revel in the chaos he had unleashed, his dark smile now transformed into a grimace of sadistic delight. Christopher's jaw tightened as he recognized him as the source of the sudden violence that had shattered the mourning ceremony.

With a steely resolve, Christopher began weaving through the chaos, using gravestones and mausoleums as cover. His training allowed him to move swiftly and efficiently, his mind focused on neutralizing the threat and protecting the innocent bystanders caught in the crossfire.

As bullets zipped through the air, Christopher remained vigilant, his senses attuned to every sound and movement. The scent of gunpowder mingled with the earthy aroma of freshly dug graves, creating a disorienting sensory overload. But amidst the chaos, his determination burned like an unwavering flame, driving him forward.

His sights locked onto the sinister man, who seemed to effortlessly evade the chaos he had orchestrated. Christopher's finger tightened around the trigger, his aim steady and unwavering. He knew that in this moment, he had to act decisively, before more innocent lives were endangered.

With a controlled burst of gunfire, Christopher unleashed a volley of shots, seeking to neutralize the threat before him. The cracks of his weapon intermingled with the symphony of chaos, echoing through the cemetery as each bullet found its mark.

But the man proved to be elusive, his movements swift and evasive. He seemed to possess an unnatural agility, darting between tombstones and mausoleums like a shadow. Christopher gritted his teeth, refusing to let frustration consume him. He adjusted his strategy, relying on his instincts and training to outmanoeuvre his adversary.

As the gunfire continued, Christopher's focus remained unyielding. He constantly reassessed his surroundings, ensuring the safety of the innocent bystanders who had sought refuge amidst the chaos. His movements were deliberate, and calculated, as he sought to end the violence that threatened to consume the cemetery.

The acrid scent of gun smoke hung heavy in the air, mingling with the scent of rain that had begun to fall, the droplets poured heavily on the earth. Disrupting the zipping sound of bullets and cries of fleeing mourners with its thunderous downpour. However, Christopher pressed on, his determination unyielding, his resolve unshakeable. He knew that in this moment, his actions held the weight of lives in the balance.

As he closed in on his target, Christopher's heart pounded in his chest, a mix of adrenaline and duty coursing through his veins. His finger tightened on the trigger again, ready to confront the sinister man and end the violence that had disrupted this solemn gathering.

In that chaotic moment, Christopher embodied the epitome of a protector, remained of the unfortunate events of his mother's demise and driven by a sense of justice and a commitment to safeguarding the innocent. The rain fell harder now, drenching the cemetery in a cleansing torrent, as if nature sought to wash away the darkness that had marred this gathering.

As the chaos of the firefight continued to unfold, Christopher's attention was abruptly diverted as Briggs, his trusted partner, approached him with a sense of urgency. The gravity of Briggs' words struck him like a physical blow. They had been surrounded, their escape routes cut off, leaving them trapped amid a dangerous and volatile situation.

Without hesitation, Christopher assessed the blood at the side of Briggs' head, his concern mounting. Time seemed to slow as he quickly processed the severity of the situation. Briggs' injury was a stark reminder of the real and immediate danger they faced.

Gripping his gun tightly, Christopher's mind raced, searching for a way to ensure their survival and navigate the perilous circumstances they found themselves in. The weight of the situation bore down upon him, fuelling his determination to protect himself and his wounded partner.

"Can you walk?" Christopher asked urgently, his voice laced with concern and determination. He knew they needed to regroup, to find a safer vantage point where they could assess the situation and formulate a plan of action.

Briggs, though visibly weakened by his injury, nodded resolutely. His eyes, filled with pain and determination, conveyed his unwavering commitment to their mission. Despite the blood staining his temple, he was determined not to let it hinder their escape.

Christopher's instincts kicked into overdrive as he swiftly guided Briggs, supporting him with an arm around his waist. They moved quickly, seeking the cover of nearby tombstones and monuments, using the chaotic environment to their advantage.

As they manoeuvred through the treacherous landscape, the gunfire continued to echo through the air, punctuated by sporadic screams and shouts. Christopher's senses remained sharp, his awareness heightened as he constantly scanned their surroundings, searching for any sign of an escape route or an opportunity to get to their car parked in the distance.

Fortunately for them, the men shooting seem to have run out of bullets and began reloading. This was the perfect time for Christopher and Briggs to move. They sprinted so fast and got to their car.

As Christopher and Briggs scrambled into the car, the situation's urgency weighed heavily upon them. Christopher swiftly took his place behind the wheel, his hands gripping the steering wheel tightly as he assessed their surroundings. A sense of foreboding washed over him as he glanced forward through the front window and back at the back window, confirming their worst fears – they were completely surrounded.

His gaze locked onto the row of men in black suits and dark sunglasses, an intimidating sight that sent a chill down his spine. The heavy weaponry they brandished was a stark reminder of the danger that awaited them. These were not ordinary adversaries; they were highly trained and well-equipped individuals who would stop at nothing to prevent Christopher and Briggs from escaping.

The tension in the air was palpable as the men maintained their steely gaze, their faces impassive behind the shield of their shades. It was clear that they had been meticulously positioned, strategically placed to obstruct any escape attempt. Christopher's heart raced, his mind racing to devise a plan to outmanoeuvre their pursuers and ensure their survival.

With a calculated sense of urgency, Christopher started the engine, the roar of the car's motor blending with the adrenaline coursing through his veins. As he shifted gears, his gaze remained fixed on the line of armed men, studying their positions, searching for any sign of weakness or opportunity. Each second felt like an eternity as he waited for the perfect moment to seize their chance at escape.

With sudden acceleration, Christopher manoeuvred the car, expertly navigating the narrow space between the caskets and the men who stood in their way. Tires screeched against the unforgiving pavement as the vehicle shot forward, narrowly avoiding the encircling net of danger.

The men in black suits reacted swiftly, their training evident as they began to give chase. Christopher's heart pounded as he deftly weaved through the labyrinthine cemetery, utilizing every ounce of his driving skill to elude their relentless pursuers.

The atmosphere inside the car was thick with tension, Briggs gripped the seat tightly, his injured head throbbing in pain. Christopher's mind raced, strategizing their next move, searching to shake off their determined adversaries and find a safe haven.

As the car careened around a sharp turn, Christopher caught a glimpse of an alleyway up ahead. It offered a potential escape route, a narrow passage that could provide the cover they desperately needed. With a deft manoeuvre, he swerved into the alley, the car's tires gripping the pavement with determination.

Behind them, the sound of screeching tires and shouts filled the air, signalling the relentless pursuit of their adversaries. Christopher's grip on the steering wheel tightened, his focus unwavering as he navigated the tight confines of the alleyway. Shadows danced across the car's windows, casting an ominous veil over their desperate flight.

As they gained distance from their pursuers, Christopher's mind raced, considering their options. He knew they needed to regroup, to find a place of relative safety where they could tend to Briggs' injuries and devise a plan to confront the larger threat that loomed over them.

Minutes later, the car stopped between towering buildings in a secluded parking lot. Christopher quickly turned off the engine, the sudden silence filling the air. He glanced at Briggs, concern etched on his face as he assessed his partner's condition.

"We need to patch you up," Christopher said, his voice filled with determination. But Briggs did not respond. He quickly turned to Briggs to see if he was okay. But Briggs looked half conscious and half unconscious. His face was pale but resolute. Knowing this was not good Christopher pressed his leg against the accelerator and zoomed off to a nearby hospital.

Amid the chaos and uncertainty, Briggs found solace in the confines of his dream, a brief respite from the dangers surrounding him. As sleep embraced him, he was transported to a familiar, comforting place—a warm, comfortable bachelor's den.

The room radiated with a cosy ambience, suffused with the soft glow of dimmed lights. Smooth jazz filled the air, its melodic notes creating a soothing backdrop to the scene. In the corner of the room, a record player spun gently, its dulcet tunes weaving a tapestry of nostalgia.

Briggs found himself in the arms of Racheal, in this dream-like dance. Her presence exuded elegance and sensuality, her flawless skin illuminated by the warm hues of the room. As they swayed and twirled to the rhythm of the music, time seemed to slow, allowing them to savour each moment.

He revelled in the feeling of her body pressed against his, the familiarity of their connection providing a sanctuary from the harsh realities of their lives. In this dream, Briggs could let go of his burdens, immersing himself in the simple pleasure of the dance, lost in the enchantment of the moment.

The subtle fragrance of her perfume filled the air, mingling with the rich aroma of the scotch in his glass. Its amber hue caught the light, casting an inviting glow. Briggs took a sip of scotch, relishing the smoothness as it danced across his palate, the warmth of the drink infusing him with a sense of comfort and relaxation.

Briggs marvelled at Racheal's grace and beauty as they moved in perfect harmony. Her laughter resonated like music, a melody that harmonized with the swaying rhythm of their bodies. The world outside the den seemed distant, faded into insignificance as he immersed himself in the joy of this dreamlike moment.

In the embrace of the dance, time ceased to exist. Briggs and Racheal became the sole inhabitants of their private sanctuary, their bodies entwined in a language that transcended words. Their every movement spoke of desire and connection, an unspoken understanding that bound them together.

As the music swelled, their dance became more passionate, their bodies moving in sync, their souls intertwining. Briggs revelled in the sensation of Racheal's touch, her warmth seeping into his very being. In this dream, the world faded away, leaving only the two of them, wrapped in an embrace that transcended the confines of reality.

But even within the dream, a whisper of reality lingered. Briggs knew that this blissful respite was temporary, a fleeting escape from the perils of the world outside. Yet, for this moment, he allowed himself to be consumed by the dream, to find solace in its embrace.

The music played in his head as Christopher zoomed off the wet road. It wove its magic, offering a glimpse into a life untouched by danger and uncertainty.

Briggs cherished this dream, clinging to its fleeting embrace. It served as a reminder of the life he longed for, a life where simplicity, warmth, and love prevailed. And though the dream would fade, leaving only fragments of its enchantment, it offered a glimmer of hope, a beacon of light in the darkness that awaited him when he awoke.

CHAPTER FIVE

As Briggs gradually regained consciousness, he found himself in a hospital room, surrounded by the sterile environment of white walls and the scent of antiseptic. His head throbbed with a sharp pain, a reminder of his ordeal. Confusion swept over him as he tried to make sense of his surroundings.

Wincing, he propped himself up in the bed, taking in his surroundings. His gaze fell upon the unfamiliar operation gown he was wearing, its fabric rustling softly as he shifted. The rhythmic beeping of the monitoring equipment filled the room, intermingling with the distant sounds of hospital activity.

Briggs's hand instinctively reached for his head, seeking to alleviate the ache that pulsed through his skull. As he did, he noticed the intravenous drip connected to his arm, delivering fluids and medication. Determined to regain control, he carefully unhooked himself from the medical apparatus, his movements filled with urgency and determination.

In that moment, Christopher entered the room, his presence a welcome sight. The lines of worry etched across his face spoke volumes about the severity of their situation. Racheal followed closely behind him, concern evident in her eyes.

Christopher's gaze met Briggs's, a mixture of relief and caution in his expression. Briggs could sense that there was much to discuss, secrets and revelations that needed to be shared. But as he spotted Racheal, his whole concerns got swept off.

"Thank goodness you're awake Mr. Briggs" Christopher said, his voice laced with relief and urgency. "You had us worried there for a moment. How are you feeling?"

Briggs's voice was hoarse as he replied, "Head hurts like hell, but I'll live. What happened?"

Christopher's brows furrowed as he recounted the events. "After you collapsed during the chaos at the cemetery, I managed to get you to safety. We called for an ambulance, and they brought you here. The doctors said you suffered a concussion and needed immediate medical attention."

Briggs nodded, the memories slowly piecing together. Racheal stepped forward, and her eyes matched his gaze.

As Briggs and Racheal locked eyes, a silent conversation unfolded between them, the weight of their unspoken words hanging in the air. In that moment of connection, myriad emotions swirled within their gaze. Anger, love, longing, and a tinge of vulnerability were all present, entangled in their silent exchange.

Briggs could feel his heart pounding in his chest, a mixture of anticipation and uncertainty. Rachael's penetrating gaze seemed to lay bare his soul, leaving him feeling exposed and self-conscious. He could sense the depth of their shared history, the unspoken words and untold stories between them.

Christopher, ever perceptive, recognized the weight of the moment and the need for privacy. Sensing the palpable tension in the room, he quietly excused himself, so his departure could create a space for Briggs and Racheal to confront their emotions.

Once alone, the room seemed to shrink, their surroundings fading into the background as their connection intensified. Briggs shifted uncomfortably under Rachael's penetrating gaze, his mind racing to find the right words to break the silence that enveloped them.

Finally, finding his voice, Briggs spoke, his words laced with vulnerability and determination. "Rachael, I... I'm sorry for everything. For the way things ended between us, for the pain I caused you."

As Racheal stood before Briggs, her once angry gaze melted off to a gaze filled with a mixture of determination and tenderness, she began with a sigh.

"Briggs..." Rachael's eyes softened, revealing the depth of her emotions. She spoke softly, her voice carrying a trace of sadness and longing.

Her words hung in the air, pregnant with unspoken desires and unresolved emotions. Briggs's heart ached at her voice's raw honesty, his longing echoing. Their distance seemed unbearable, as if an invisible force kept them apart.

With a mixture of trepidation and determination, Briggs reached out, his hand gently grazing Rachael's. Their fingers intertwined, a tangible connection that bridged the gap between them. He pulled her to the bed where he sat, and she sat beside him.

At that moment, words became superfluous as their gaze spoke volumes. The room seemed to fade away, leaving only the palpable tension and the unspoken promises between them.

Racheal's expression softened as her gaze shifted to the drip he had hastily removed from his hand. She moved closer to him, her touch gentle and familiar as she carefully reconnected the tubing.

A realisation struck as Briggs reflected on the circumstances that led him to be hospitalised. Racheal, being a nurse, was likely the reason why Christopher had rushed him to this hospital. He had an aversion to taking medications and how they had been a contention between them.

In the past, Racheal had always been there to ensure he took his prescribed medications. She understood the importance of adhering to the treatment plan and the potential consequences of neglecting his health. Despite his resistance, she had been unwavering in her commitment to his well-being.

She had always known how to navigate his resistance, reminding him of the importance of his health without compromising their love. Racheal's firm but caring insistence on taking his medication resurfaced in Briggs's mind. He remembered her patience, understanding, and ability to balance empathy with firmness.

He saw the same determination in her eyes as he glanced at Racheal. She had always been his advocate, ensuring he received the care he needed even when he resisted. At that moment, Briggs realized the depth of her commitment to him.

The hospital room faded into the background as Briggs focused on the woman before him. He felt a surge of gratitude for her presence in his life, her unwavering dedication, and her understanding of his complexities.

Without uttering a word, Briggs reached out and gently clasped Racheal's hand in his own again. In that hospital room, surrounded by the beeping monitors and the scent of antiseptic, Briggs found comfort in the presence of the woman who understood him like no one else.

The door opened, and Christopher entered the room with Bretty in tow, Briggs couldn't hide his displeasure at the sight of her. He was still sceptical about her intentions and didn't trust her completely. However, as Bretty spoke up and asked for a chance to be heard, he reluctantly agreed to listen.

Bretty took a deep breath and began explaining herself to Briggs, her voice filled with urgency and determination. 'Durango and his men were planning to leave town that moment with a secret weapon they had obtained from Tony. Their destination was America. They intended to execute a series of devastating attacks on innocent citizens.'

Bretty trembled as she emphasised the gravity of the situation, 'The weapon in question is highly dangerous and had the potential to cause widespread destruction. If Durango and his men could carry out their plans, it would result in an immense loss of life and irreparable damage.'

Bretty pleaded with Briggs to understand the urgency and the significance of capturing Durango that night. She stressed that if they could corner Durango and his men, there was a high possibility of stopping their immediate threat and gaining valuable information about the terrorist group they were associated with.

She shared details she had overheard during her time with Tony, snippets of conversations and hints that pointed towards a larger network operating behind the scenes. Bretty explained that Durango was not just an isolated individual but a key player in a dangerous organization that posed a significant threat to national security.

Briggs listened intently, his scepticism gradually fading as he absorbed the weight of Bretty's words. He recognized the gravity of the situation and the potential consequences of letting Durango and his men escape. Despite his initial reservations, he realized they couldn't afford to ignore this opportunity to gather vital intelligence and prevent further harm.

Reluctantly, Briggs nodded, acknowledging the urgency of the mission. He understood that capturing Durango that night was their best chance to unravel the intricate web of terror and protect innocent lives. It was a race against time, and Briggs knew they had to act swiftly and decisively.

Rachel glanced back and forth between Bretty and Briggs, her face contorted with fear and disapproval. With a heavy heart, Briggs could sense her apprehension and understood the weight of her concerns.

Their eyes locked, and Briggs held his breath, knowing he had to address Rachel's fears. He reached for her hand, squeezing it gently as he spoke with a determined yet reassuring tone.

"You know I have to go, Ray," he said softly, his voice filled with a mix of conviction and love. "I promise I will do everything I can to ensure my safety. But if we don't stop Durango and his men now, countless innocent lives will be at risk. We can't turn a blind eye to this threat."

Rachel's eyes welled with tears, and tightened her grip on Briggs' hand. The fear of losing him weighed heavily on her, but she knew deep down that his commitment to protecting others was a fundamental part of his identity.

She released her drip from him quickly and stood up with a mixture of sadness and frustration etched on her face. She couldn't bear to see Briggs willingly putting himself in harm's way again. Without saying a word, she turned and swiftly left the room, leaving Christopher, Bretty, and Briggs behind.

As Briggs watched her retreat from the room, his heart sank, knowing he had again caused her pain. Christopher and Bretty remained seated on the bed, their expressions mirroring the gravity of the situation.

Silence enveloped the room as Briggs processed Rachel's departure. He knew their relationship had already been strained by the dangers he faced in his work. The constant threat to his life had taken its toll on both of them, leaving Rachel torn between her love for Briggs and the fear of losing him.

Bretty broke the silence, her voice laced with sympathy. "She's scared, Briggs. Scared of losing you, scared of the risks you take. We all are, to some extent."

Christopher turned to Briggs, his eyes filled with determination. Despite the tension in the room caused by Rachel's departure, he remained focused on the task. He spoke firmly with a sense of urgency, his voice carrying a steely resolve.

"If we move fast, Briggs, we can catch up with Durango's men and apprehend them," Christopher declared, his tone resolute. "We can't let this opportunity slip through our fingers. Lives are at stake, and we can stop them."

Briggs nodded, acknowledging the truth in Christopher's words. They couldn't afford to hesitate because it was a race against time.

"You're right, Christopher," Briggs responded, determination resurfacing in his voice.

Briggs and Christopher stood in a dimly lit room, the air heavy with anticipation. They had meticulously laid out various weapons on a sturdy table, carefully selecting their armaments for the upcoming ambush. Each item held its own purpose, a tool of defence and offence in their mission to apprehend Durango and his men.

With grim determination etched on their faces, Briggs and Christopher equipped themselves. They donned tactical jackets, their hands moving swiftly yet methodically to secure the weapons in concealed pockets, holsters, and belts. The weight of the arsenal added an extra layer of gravity to their already tense demeanour.

Briggs selected a compact handgun, sliding it into a shoulder holster hidden beneath his jacket. He strapped a combat knife to his ankle, ensuring it was easily accessible. With practised precision, he loaded spare ammunition into his pockets, ready to reload swiftly in the heat of the impending confrontation.

Meanwhile, Christopher chose a different approach, opting for a larger weapon. He attached a submachine gun to a sling across his chest, the weapon resting comfortably against his body. He carefully tucked spare magazines into his vest, ensuring quick access to additional rounds. A utility belt adorned with various tools and gadgets completed his ensemble, ready to assist in any tactical situation.

As they armed themselves, their focus remained unwavering, their minds consumed with the imminent danger ahead.

Silent determination radiated between the two men as they continued their preparations.

Christopher broke the silence, his voice filled with hope and vulnerability. He turned to Briggs, their eyes meeting in a moment of shared determination.

"You know, Briggs," Christopher began, his tone tinged with a hint of exhaustion, "we've been chasing shadows for the past three months. Every lead we've followed has ended up as a dead-end or an unconnected detail. It's been frustrating, to say the least."

Briggs nodded. The case they had been investigating had proven to be an enigma, a complex puzzle with pieces that seemed to slip through their fingers. The constant setbacks had fallen on their morale, sowing doubt in their minds.

"I won't lie," Christopher continued, his voice tinged with a hint of discouragement. "I was starting to lose faith. But when Bretty showed up, and with the information she has, and this new possibility of finally cornering Durango and uncovering the truth, I feel a glimmer of hope."

Briggs leaned against the table, contemplating Christopher's words. He shared his partner's sentiment. The case had consumed their lives, and the lack of progress had become disheartening.

"I understand, Chris," Briggs responded, calm yet resolute. "We've been on this rollercoaster for far too long. Maybe Bretty was the missing piece we've been searching for. Just maybe"

Christopher's eyes brightened at Briggs' words, a renewed determination igniting him. He had known Briggs long enough to recognize the unwavering intuition that guided his partner's instincts. If Briggs believed in the potential breakthrough, Christopher would stand by him, ready to seize the opportunity.

"I have faith, too," Christopher admitted, a note of conviction resonating in his voice. "Bretty's connection to Tony, her firsthand knowledge of his operations, it's invaluable. If we can apprehend Durango tonight, we might finally get the break we've been waiting for."

Briggs nodded in agreement, a glimmer of optimism creeping into his eyes.

Briggs looked at Christopher, his gaze steady and contemplative. He took a moment to absorb his partner's words before responding, his voice filled with determination and caution.

"I hope so too, Chris," Briggs said, his tone laced with anticipation. "Still we can't be too careful"

He paused, taking a deep breath before continuing. "I've reached out to Alexander Q, and he's agreed to send his men as backup for this mission. He wants Durango alive and willing to do whatever it takes to bring him to justice."

Christopher's eyebrows raised a mix of relief and gratitude washing over his face. The prospect of having additional support from Alexander Q's team was a game-changer, potentially tipping the scales in their favour.

"That's a major boost," Christopher acknowledged, his voice filled with a renewed sense of hope. "Durango won't slip through our fingers this time."

"But we have to remember," Briggs cautioned, his voice filled with a sense of realism, "our primary objective is to capture Durango alive. We must gather as much information as possible to dismantle the entire network."

Christopher nodded in agreement. He understood that capturing Durango would be the first step in unravelling the intricate web of criminal activities that plagued their city.

"Together, with the backup from Alexander Q's team, we can make it happen," Christopher affirmed, his voice brimming with determination. "This is our chance to bring justice to those affected by Durango's actions and end the reign of terror."

Briggs shared a nod of agreement and took a deep breath, the weight of recent discoveries heavy on his mind. He turned to Christopher, a determined expression etched on his face.

"Chris, remember the clues we found at Thomas' basement?' Briggs began, his voice tinged with a mix of gravity and urgency. Christopher nodded 'Well, it has shed some light on the situation," Briggs continued "Alexander's team thoroughly investigated the evidence, and it appears that Thomas is connected to this terrorist cell."

Christopher's mind struggled to process the revelation. Thomas, a trusted agent in the Secret Intelligence Service (SIS), being linked to the very group they were investigating was a shocking twist.

"Thomas? But he's been working with us all along," Christopher said, his voice tinged with disbelief. "How could he be involved in this?"

Briggs nodded. The betrayal was palpable, and the implications were significant. He had been in this line of work so long it no longer strike him as hard. He continued to explain the situation as he knew it.

"The agency believes Thomas may be a double agent, working for this terrorist cell while seemingly operating within the SIS," Briggs explained. "He has been apprehended and is currently undergoing interrogation to ascertain the extent of his involvement."

Christopher absorbed the information, his mind racing with questions and conflicting emotions. The trust they had placed in Thomas, their reliance on his expertise, now felt shattered.

"I can't believe it," Christopher muttered, a mix of disappointment and frustration in his voice. "We trusted him, worked alongside him. How could we have been so blind?"

Briggs placed a reassuring hand on Christopher's back, offering support and encouragement.

"Chris, we mustn't lose sight of the bigger picture. Discovering Thomas' involvement, no matter how unsettling, is progress."

He looked into Christopher's eyes, the intensity of his gaze conveying a shared determination. "We may feel like we're going around in circles, but uncovering these connections brings us closer to unravelling the truth. We're making progress, even if it's not always apparent."

Christopher sighed, slowly absorbing Briggs' words. He recognized the truth in his partner's reassurance despite the shock and disillusionment.

"You're right, Briggs," Christopher said, his voice tinged with newfound determination. "We can't let this setback discourage us. We must keep pushing forward, no matter how challenging the road ahead may be."

Briggs smiled, a mixture of pride and camaraderie shining in his eyes. "That's the spirit, Chris. We've come too far to give up now. We'll get to the bottom of this. We'll bring down the entire network, and ensure justice is served."

Christopher couldn't help but notice the sadness in Briggs' eyes, a glint of hidden pain mirrored his own. They had been partners for years, and though they had shared countless dangerous missions, Briggs rarely spoke about his personal life. Yet, Christopher knew enough to understand that the current situation was taking a toll on Briggs and his relationship with Racheal.

Briggs and Racheal had been together for a decade, a testament to their enduring bond in a world of uncertainty and danger. They had weathered storms, faced their own demons, and emerged stronger together. But this time, the darkness that loomed over their lives seemed insurmountable, threatening to tear them apart.

Christopher recalled the moments he had witnessed between Briggs and Racheal, the stolen glances, the small gestures of affection that spoke volumes about their love. They had always found solace in each other's arms, a sanctuary amidst the chaos of their work. But now, the weight of their circumstances seemed pushing them further apart, creating an impenetrable divide.

As Christopher considered the depth of their relationship, he couldn't help but feel a pang of empathy for his partner. He understood the sacrifices they all made in service of their duty, the toll it took on personal relationships. It was a constant struggle to balance their professional responsibilities and personal lives, and sometimes, it seemed impossible to reconcile the two.

But this case, with its intricate web of deceit and danger, had brought them to a breaking point. The stakes were higher than ever, and the consequences of failure were unimaginable. It was no wonder the strain was taking its toll on Briggs and Racheal's relationship.

Christopher was aware of the future that Briggs envisioned with Racheal. He knew all too well how much his partner loved and cherished her. Their quieter conversations revealed Briggs' desire to leave behind the dangerous life they led and create a peaceful existence for himself and Racheal.

Briggs had often spoken about retirement, a word that carried with it a sense of hope and relief to him. Christopher had witnessed the way Briggs' eyes would light up as he painted vivid pictures of a life away from the constant danger and uncertainty of their work. He dreamed of quiet mornings with Racheal, sipping coffee together as they watched the sunrise, and lazy afternoons spent exploring new places, hand in hand.

The thought of retiring and giving Racheal the life she deserved kept Briggs going during the darkest moments of their missions. The beacon of light guided him through the storms, a constant reminder of the love and happiness he longed to provide for Racheal.

Racheal was the light that illuminated his world, the very essence of his happiness. Briggs would stop at nothing to protect her, to shield her from harm, and to provide her with a life of peace and contentment. Briggs' unwavering love and devotion for Racheal was unreal.

Racheal was not only Briggs' partner but also his anchor, the source of his strength and motivation. Her smile could dissolve the world's weight from his shoulders, and her touch could heal the wounds their line of work inflicted upon his soul. She was his sanctuary, his refuge from the chaos that surrounded them.

Christopher understood that Briggs saw anyone or anything that threatened Racheal's well-being as an archenemy, an adversary to be confronted and defeated. The fierce determination in Briggs' eyes whenever Racheal's safety was at stake was unmistakable. He would move mountains and face insurmountable odds to ensure her happiness and protect her from harm.

The desire to retire and give Racheal the life she deserved was a driving force for Briggs. It fuelled his every action and decision, pushing him forward even when the mission seemed insurmountable. The thought of finally leaving behind the dangerous world they inhabited and embracing a tranquil existence with Racheal kept his spirits high in times of adversity.

However, the current mission seemed to be expanding beyond their initial expectations. It was testing their limits and challenging their resolve. The path they had embarked upon was fraught with danger and uncertainty, with each step leading them deeper into a complex web of deception and treachery.

While he understood Briggs' burning desire to retire and give Racheal the life she deserved, he also recognized the importance of completing their current assignment. They couldn't turn a blind eye to the threat that loomed over innocent lives and the potential devastation that awaited if they failed.

In their line of work, sacrifices were often necessary, and personal desires sometimes had to be put on hold for the greater good. Christopher knew that Briggs carried this burden heavily on his shoulders, torn between his love for Racheal and his duty to protect the innocent.

Briggs and Christopher stepped outside, commanding attention as they met Bretty. She stood there, clad in a sleek, form-fitting leather suit that exuded a sense of strength and confidence. Her eyes met theirs, a shared understanding passing between them.

Without uttering a word, Bretty nodded at both men, acknowledging their readiness for the upcoming mission. There was an air of determination about her, a focused energy that mirrored the intensity burning within Briggs and Christopher.

As they walked towards the waiting car, the tension in the air was palpable. Briggs took the driver's seat, his strong hands firmly gripping the steering wheel. Christopher and Bretty settled in the back, focused on the task. The engine roared to life, its rumble cutting through the silence as they embarked on the path leading them to their target.

As the car surged forward, the city lights blurred into streaks of colour, mirroring the urgency that propelled them forward. The road stretched out before them, winding and unpredictable, much like the path they had chosen to take. They were acutely aware that danger lurked around every corner, but they were determined to see justice served.

As the car continued to traverse the road, Briggs took a moment to go through the intricacies of their plan.

Briggs turned his attention to Bretty, acknowledging her familiarity with Durango's facility. Her role was crucial in initiating the diversion that would create a momentary distraction to Durango's men. Bretty's confidence and expertise made her the perfect candidate to lead this operation.

With a resolute voice, Briggs outlined Bretty's task. She would enter the facility first, stealthily manoeuvring through the shadows, leaving a trail of disruption in her wake. Her mission was to sow chaos, to distract Durango's men, and divert their attention away from the impending assault.

On the other hand, Christopher had a pivotal role in disabling the power supply to the facility. With the darkness as their ally, Durango's men would be disoriented and unable to effectively utilize their weapons. Christopher's technology and strategic thinking expertise made him the perfect candidate for this task. He would infiltrate the powerhouse, shutting down the systems and plunging the facility into darkness.

Briggs emphasized the importance of timing, stressing the need for synchronization between Bretty's diversion and Christopher's disruption. They had to strike swiftly and efficiently, catching their enemies off guard and preventing them from retaliating effectively. The element of surprise was their greatest advantage.

As the plan unfolded, Alexander Q's men would make their move. They would storm the facility, taking advantage of the chaos and darkness, catching Durango's men unaware. Their objective was to neutralize the threat swiftly and effectively, disable Durango and his men to get the weapon before they transport...

Briggs knew the stakes were high, and success relied on every team member playing their part flawlessly. He stressed the importance of coordination and communication, reminding everyone of the risks they were undertaking.

With the plan now solidified, the car moved steadily towards their destination. The road stretched before them, each passing mile bringing them closer to their moment of reckoning. The atmosphere in the car was a mix of anticipation and resolve, a shared understanding that their actions would shape the outcome of this mission.

Upon reaching their destination, they took a moment to assess the surroundings. The facility appeared quiet and seemingly undisturbed, with no immediate signs of activity. The anticipation weighed heavily as they prepared to set their plan in motion.

Briggs took charge, laying out the final details of their strategy. He emphasized the importance of timing and coordination, stressing the need for stealth and precision. They all understood the gravity of the situation and the potential consequences if they failed.

With their roles defined, they stepped out of the car, their steps purposeful and determined. Each team member knew their part and the critical role they played in the mission's success. The night air was cool, and the silence only added to the tension that filled their minds.

Briggs signalled for Bretty to move forward, her expertise and familiarity with the facility making her the ideal candidate for creating a diversion. Dressed in her sleek leather suit, she nodded in acknowledgement before disappearing into the darkness, blending into the shadows like a phantom.

Christopher and Briggs shared a brief nod, their unspoken understanding fuelling their determination. They began their silent approach towards the facility with their weapons discreetly concealed within their attire.

As they neared the entrance, their senses heightened, attuned to any sign of danger or movement. The moonlight cast faint shadows, providing them with a modicum of cover. Their heartbeats quickened, synchronized in rhythm as they prepared themselves mentally and emotionally for the imminent challenge.

Christopher's focus shifted towards the powerhouse, knowing that disabling the facility's power supply would be pivotal. He meticulously navigated the darkened terrain, mindful of potential obstacles hindering his progress. His agile movements betrayed years of training and experience.

On the other hand, Briggs slipped into the facility's perimeter, his steps barely audible against the concrete floor. The stillness enveloped him, adding an eerie quality to the atmosphere. His instincts guided him, leading him deeper into the labyrinthine structure, his eyes scanning every corner and alcove.

He moved with calculated precision, an air of anticipation hung in the balance. The silence was palpable, pregnant with the impending storm of action and uncertainty. The tension tightened like a coiled spring, ready to unleash its energy upon the first spark of chaos.

As Briggs weaved through the maze of crates, his thoughts became consumed by the whispers he had overheard during the funeral procession. The gravity of their words lingered in his mind, teasing his curiosity and stirring his determination to uncover the truth.

The notion of a double agent within the ranks of the SIS and CIA sent a shiver down Briggs' spine. It meant that their enemy had a powerful ally working from within, with access to vital information and the ability to manipulate events to their advantage. Briggs couldn't help but wonder who this mysterious person could be, and how deeply they were embedded in the intelligence agencies.

He pondered the possibilities, his mind running through the list of familiar faces he had encountered throughout his career. Was it someone he trusted, someone he had worked closely with? Or perhaps it was someone whose true intentions had been carefully concealed beneath a facade of loyalty and duty.

The weight of suspicion pressed upon Briggs as he considered the implications. He knew uncovering the double agent's identity was crucial for their mission's success.

Briggs' thoughts circled back to the funeral and the gathering of agents and their families. The faces of his colleagues and their loved ones flashed before his eyes, and he couldn't help but question each one in his mind. Was the traitor possibly standing among them, hiding in plain sight?

He pushed these thoughts aside for the moment, recognizing that his primary objective was to locate and apprehend Durango. With each step he took, Briggs remained physically and mentally vigilant. He knew that the answers he sought lay within the chaos awaiting him. The mission had become more complex, the stakes higher than ever, but Briggs was prepared to face whatever challenges lay ahead.

The sudden blackout sent shockwaves of urgency through his veins as Briggs manoeuvred through the dimly lit facility. The darkness amplified the chaos, allowing him to blend seamlessly with the shadows as he embraced the element of surprise. The cacophony of gunshots and frantic shouts echoed through the air, creating a symphony of turmoil that drowned out any semblance of order.

Briggs navigated the treacherous terrain with calculated precision. The sporadic bursts of gunfire served as his guiding beacon, drawing him towards the heart of the conflict. He moved swiftly, his senses heightened as he evaded stray bullets and dived behind crates for cover.

Amidst the turmoil, he caught glimpses of Alexander Q's men infiltrating the facility. They moved like a well-oiled machine, their tactical expertise evident in their synchronized movements and strategic positioning. Their presence injected a renewed sense of purpose into Briggs' mission, as he realized he was not alone in this fight.

The intermingling of darkness and chaos created a surreal atmosphere, intensifying Briggs' focus and sharpening his senses. He relied on his instincts to make split-second decisions amidst the pandemonium. Every step brought him closer to his target, as he skilfully maneuvered through the labyrinth of crates and machinery.

The deafening sound of gunshots and the acrid smell of gunpowder filled the air, fuelling Briggs' determination. Amidst the chaos, Briggs remained steadfast, his mind focused on the task at hand. The adrenaline coursing through his veins propelled him forward, his movements becoming a seamless dance between stealth and aggression. He engaged in sporadic firefights, skilfully neutralizing threats while continuing his relentless pursuit.

As the battle raged, Briggs caught glimpses of Durango's men, their desperate attempts to regroup and defend their stronghold. Their disarray gave Briggs an advantage, allowing him to exploit their vulnerabilities and move undetected towards his ultimate target.

Time seemed to distort in the darkness, with each passing second feeling eternal and fleeting. But Briggs pushed forward, undeterred by fatigue or the chaos around him. His unwavering resolve propelled him through the perils in his path, his mind honed on his singular objective.

Finally, through a haze of smoke and shattered crates, Briggs caught sight of Durango. The man exuded an air of menace, his eyes flickering with desperation and determination. Briggs knew this was the defining moment of their encounter, the culmination of months of investigation and pursuit.

As Briggs carefully weaved through the darkness, the chaos around him became a swirling maelstrom of violence and panic. Bullets whizzed past him, the crackling sounds filling the air, as screams and shouts reverberated throughout the facility. Each step he took was measured, every movement calculated to ensure his approach remained undetected.

The sporadic flickering of muzzle flashes illuminated the scene sporadically, providing brief glimpses of the ongoing battle. Briggs utilized these fleeting moments of light to assess his surroundings, quickly adapting his path to avoid direct confrontation and stay hidden.

His heart pounded in his chest, adrenaline coursing through his veins as he closed in on Durango. The weight of the mission pressed upon him, driving him forward with a singular focus. The importance of apprehending Durango weighed heavily on his mind, knowing that the safety of countless lives depended on his success.

Briggs maintained his silence, breathing steady as he moved closer to his target. He used the chaos as his cloak, taking advantage of the distractions provided by the ongoing firefight to inch ever closer to Durango's position.

The darkness became his ally, obscuring his presence as he stealthily approached Durango from behind. Every instinct honed through years of training guided him, allowing him to navigate the hazardous terrain without stumbling or giving away his position.

As he closed the distance, the sounds of the battle grew louder, drowning out any noise he might make. His muscles tensed, ready to strike at the opportune moment. His fingers gripped the handle of his weapon tightly, his mind focused on the mission.

Finally, he was mere steps away from Durango. Sweat beaded on his forehead as he braced himself for the crucial moment. With utmost precision and speed, Briggs lunged forward, his hand reaching out to grab Durango from behind. The element of surprise was on his side, and Durango, caught off guard, was momentarily paralyzed with shock.

Their bodies collided, and for a brief moment, the two men grappled in the darkness. Briggs employed close-quarters combat techniques to subdue Durango. The struggle was fierce, each man fighting for their respective cause.

As the tussle continued, Briggs fought to maintain control, leveraging his strength and agility to gain the upper hand. His determination burned bright within him, as he knew this moment could be the turning point in their relentless pursuit of justice.

However, despite his best efforts, Durango proved a formidable adversary. He wriggled and fought back, refusing to submit to Briggs' hold. Their struggle intensified, both men locked in a battle of wills, each refusing to yield.

Amid the chaos, with bullets still flying and the sounds of violence echoing around them, Durango fought back and pushed Briggs away from him to the floor. Briggs landed with a heavy thud. That moment, his pistol slide fell out of his jacket and slide next to him. Briggs quickly picked up the weapon.

As Briggs raised his weapon, his finger gently squeezing the trigger, the sudden eruption of blinding light shattered the darkness that had enveloped the facility. The intense brightness assaulted his eyes, momentarily disorienting him. He instinctively shielded his face, his vision obscured by the searing light.

As the brilliance subsided, Briggs cautiously lowered his hand, his eyes adjusting to the new environment. He found himself encircled by Durango's men, their sinister presence suffusing the air. Each bore the unmistakable coded tattoo, a mark of their allegiance to Durango's nefarious cause.

Durango stood at the centre of the gathering, a wicked smile etched across his face. His eyes glinted with triumph and malevolence, a predator revelling in his moment of control. It was a sight that made Briggs' blood run cold, realising how deeply Durango's influence had permeated the very heart of their mission.

Briggs' mind raced as he assessed the gravity of the situation. It struck him that Durango's men had anticipated their every move, and had ambushed them strategically, showing they were aware of their plans before they showed up.

Anger and frustration coursed through Briggs' veins, but he quickly stifled it. He knew that reacting impulsively would only play into Durango's hands. Instead, he maintained a calm and collected composure, a mask to conceal the storm of emotions within him.

Durango's laughter cut through the air, laced with a chilling sense of satisfaction.

As Briggs surveyed his surroundings, his heart sank at the unfolding grim scene. Most of the screams and gunfire were from Alexander Q's men, whose battered bodies now lay strewn across the floor of Durango's facility. Moans of pain and cries for help pierced the air, creating a haunting symphony of suffering.

The shock of the carnage that Durango had orchestrated struck Briggs with a force he had not anticipated. It became painfully clear that their enemy had been meticulously prepared for their arrival, expertly ambushing Alexander Q's men and turning the tables on them.

Briggs felt a surge of anger welling inside him, mingled with a profound grief. These were not just nameless soldiers; they were comrades, friends, and individuals who had volunteered to put their lives on the line to fight for what they believed in. And now, their sacrifices seemed to have been in vain.

Briggs focused on the present, suppressing his emotions, meticulously assessing the situation.

He observed the positioning of Durango's men, their strategic formation and readiness for any potential counterattack.

Durango's gaze locked onto Briggs, 'What a pleasure to finally meet you, Mr Sebastian Briggs.' His voice cutting through the air with an unexpected femininity. The stark contrast between his appearance, with a massive and menacing exterior, and his unexpectedly soft tone sent a shiver down Briggs' spine.

Briggs couldn't help but be captivated by the intricate tattoos adorned Durango's body. The ink seemed to tell a story of a dark and twisted past, each symbol etched with intention and purpose. His tattoos ran from his forehead down to his exposed chest, obscuring half of his face, and each design seemed to possess a certain mystique that amplified the aura of menace that Durango exuded.

Durango's sly smile widened as he observed Briggs' reaction, revelling in his presence's effect on his adversary. The moment hung heavy with tension as they locked eyes, both aware of the high stakes at play.

'Well, well, well, Briggs. I must say, you've caught me by surprise. I didn't expect you to walk into my lair like this.' Durango said sarcastically as he busted into laughter again. He had a thick Russian accent with a Germanic mix to it.

Briggs clutched his gun tighter in his hands.

'Oh, my dear Briggs, you underestimate the lengths I've gone to ensure your capture. I had planned to apprehend you myself, but it seems fate has brought you to me instead.' Durango said with a smirk.

'What's your grand plan, Durango? Why go to such lengths to orchestrate all this chaos?' Briggs narrowed his eyes.

Durango leaned in, his voice dripping with malice 'Ah, Briggs, my grand plan is far more intricate than you can fathom. But I suppose a small taste won't hurt. Let's just say, power is the ultimate goal. It's about time to go global don't you think?'

'You're deluded, Son. Don't you have enough of that already?'

Silence resumed back in the scene. The air crackled with tension as Briggs and Durango locked gazes, neither willing to back down. The clash of wills and the weight of their opposing objectives hung heavily

'Did you really think you were meant to survive this long? You have a friend to thank for that. A friend who would give a limb up to have you dead.'

Briggs looked confused and suspicious 'What friend are you talking about, Durango?'

Durango bursted out laughing again 'Oh, you underestimate the depth of deception, my dear Briggs. Let's just say I have a mole, a double agent in your midst. Someone close to you, someone you trust implicitly. They were the ones who set this plan into motion, to eliminate you once and for all.'

'That can't be true.' Briggs was aware of how Briggs could be a pathological liar. But it help to relieve him from being shocked.

Durango leaned in, his voice dripping with sinister delight 'Ah, but isn't that what makes betrayal so effective? The person you least suspect, the one closest to your heart, has the power to bring you down. Your friend ensured I had the information to track and plan your demise. And my men have witnessed your elusive nature firsthand. You're quite the slippery one, Briggs.'

Briggs's mind raced, trying to process this newfound revelation. Doubt and suspicion crept into his thoughts, casting a shadow over his trust in the people in his life.

'You might have to do better than that Durango. Lying is beginning to look odd on you.'

Durango smirked 'Ah, the blind loyalty of a true leader. How admirable.'

Durango's sinister laughter echoed through the room, resonating with a chilling intensity. His eyes gleamed with sadistic delight as he observed Briggs' reaction. With a deliberate movement, he reached for his wrist, unbuckling a sleek and seemingly innocuous wristwatch. He placed it on the floor and slid it across towards Briggs. He taunted him with his silence, relishing the confusion and shock etched on Briggs' face.

Briggs hesitated for a moment, his eyes fixed on the wristwatch. It was a simple device, unassuming in appearance, yet it held a weight of significance that Briggs couldn't ignore. As he picked it up, his fingers trembling slightly, his mind raced with disbelief and an overwhelming surge of emotions.

Examining the watch closely, Briggs' eyes widened in shock for a fleeting moment. The name engraved on the backplate sent a jolt of disbelief through his entire being. It was Theo's name, a dear friend and trusted ally who had met a tragic end years ago. The watch was a relic, a reminder of their shared experiences and the bond they had forged.

Struggling to process the impossible, Briggs looked up at Durango, his voice trembling with anger and desperation. "Where did you get this?"

Durango's twisted grin widened, revelling in the torment he inflicted upon Briggs. The truth remained veiled behind his enigmatic facade, and he delighted in withholding the answers Briggs desperately sought. He seemed to savour the chaos and uncertainty, knowing full well that he held the power to shatter Briggs' world.

With a cold, detached demeanour, Durango simply shrugged and offered no explanation. He relished in Briggs' torment, his silence a deliberate torment that further fuelled the fire of Briggs' anguish. The truth remained elusive, and Durango seemed to revel in the manipulation and psychological torment he inflicted upon his captive.

Anger coursed through Briggs' veins, his fists clenched in frustration. He refused to succumb to the maddening game Durango was playing. Summoning his resolve, he locked eyes with his adversary, determined to break through the wall of silence and deceit.

"Tell me, Durango," Briggs demanded, his voice laced with fury and determination. "What do you gain from this sick charade?"

Durango's expression shifted subtly, a glimmer of amusement mixed with something darker flickering in his eyes.

The room was suddenly engulfed in darkness once again. The electricity, already flickering ominously, abruptly vanished, plunging the space into a void of shadows.

Amidst the chaos, gunfire echoed through the air, reverberating with a menacing intensity. Durango's men, disoriented by the sudden darkness, fired their weapons aimlessly into the air, the sound of bullets ricocheting off metal surfaces adding to the cacophony of confusion and fear.

During the darkness and disarray, a familiar voice pierced through the chaos. Christopher's voice, filled with urgency and concern, called out to Briggs from somewhere in the darkness. "Mr Briggs! Get out of there!"

Guided by Christopher's words, Briggs swiftly manoeuvred through the maze-like corridors of Durango's facility, his heart pounding in his chest, adrenaline fuelling his every move. Each step was calculated, each turn deliberate, as he followed the trail of Christopher's voice, desperate to reach safety.

As he sprinted through the darkness, gunfire and distant screams intensified, heightening the sense of danger and urgency. Briggs' mind raced, trying to piece together the fragmented puzzle before him. Was Theo back? Was he the one who orchestrated events?

Finally, Briggs rounded a corner and found himself face-to-face with Christopher. Christopher quickly assessed the situation, his voice filled with urgency. "Briggs, we have to get out of here. Durango's men are everywhere. They're onto us."

Briggs nodded. Moving swiftly and silently, they navigated through the labyrinthine facility, avoiding the patrolling guards and taking advantage of the chaos unfolding around them. The darkness provided them with a cloak of invisibility, allowing them to slip through the shadows undetected.

As they neared the exit, their senses heightened, aware that danger lurked at every corner. The sound of alarms blaring in the distance signalled the escalation of the situation, a desperate attempt by Durango to maintain control of the chaos he had unleashed.

Finally, they burst through the doors, emerging into the cool night air. The relief was palpable. Briggs and Christopher paused for a moment, catching their breath and surveying their surroundings. They shared a brief nod, their eyes filled with determination and resolve.

They melted into the shadows, disappearing into the night.

CHAPTER SIX

The plane he and his fellow agents occupied plummeted towards the ground. The once stable aircraft now descended in a deadly spiral, its left wing engulfed in flames, casting an eerie glow across the cabin. The acrid smell of burning metal and the suffocating heat filled the air, intensifying the panic and desperation of those on board.

Briggs' heart pounded in his chest, his instincts kicking in as he fought against the turbulence, struggling to maintain balance amidst the violent jolts that shook the plane. He braced himself against the nearest solid surface, his mind racing to escape this nightmare.

Amidst the chaos, the agents on board desperately attempted to escape the impending disaster. Clutching parachutes tightly, they maneuverer through the confined space, each movement hindered by the erratic movements of the aircraft. The deafening noise of gunshots echoed through the cabin as gunfire erupted, adding a sinister layer of danger to the already dire situation.

Briggs felt the weight of his training and experience bearing down on him, propelling him forward. The memories of past missions, camaraderie and shared sacrifices, flooded his mind, interweaving with the intensity of the nightmare. He could almost hear the voices of his fallen comrades, urging him to persevere, to fight against the odds.

During the nightmarish descent, the agents turned against each other in a frenzy of violence and betrayal. The very essence of trust shattered, leaving only a vortex of bloodshed and confusion.

Briggs, still caught within the twisted realm of the dream, witnessed the horrifying spectacle. His eyes widened in disbelief and horror as he saw fellow agents, once comrades-in-arms, engaged in a deadly dance of betrayal. The unity that had once bound them together had been torn asunder, replaced by an atmosphere of treachery and deceit.

Amidst the pandemonium, a figure emerged from the shadows. Theo, a trusted ally and friend, had seemingly swayed half of the agents to his side. Theo's sinister intentions were now laid bare, his gun pointed directly at Briggs, his gaze filled with a chilling mix of malice and triumph. The arm in which he used his gun was laced with his golden wristwatch.

A sudden interruption shattered the tension-filled air as Theo prepared to pull the trigger. Agent Sasha, who had remained true to the cause, emerged from the chaos, her determination cutting through the maelstrom of violence. With a swift and decisive shot, her bullet found its mark, striking Theo's chest with precision.

Time seemed to slow as Theo's body convulsed and was propelled towards the shattered window. His figure grew smaller and smaller, disappearing into the abyss of the sky, leaving only a faint echo of his malevolence behind. It was as if the nightmare had swallowed him whole, erasing his existence from that fractured reality.

Still reeling from the shock of the betrayal, Briggs found solace in Sasha's intervention. Her act of defiance against Theo's reign of terror reminded him that amidst the darkness, there were still glimmers of hope and loyalty.

Yet, the nightmare persisted, the plane hurtling towards its catastrophic end. The impact of the crash loomed ever closer, the imminent collision with the unforgiving earth drawing nearer with each passing moment. The chaos within the plane intensified, cries of desperation and fear blending with the roar of the engines.

Amidst the chaos and impending doom, Briggs fought to regain his composure. Adrenaline surged through his veins, igniting his survival instincts and sharpening his focus. He knew he had to act swiftly and decisively to escape the nightmare.

With adrenaline coursing through his veins, Briggs lunged towards a nearby emergency exit, struggling against the force of gravity that seemed determined to pull him back into the swirling madness. With a resolute grip, he pried the door open, the rush of wind and the deafening roar of the engines swallowing the screams and cries of those around him.

The biting cold and the blinding rush of air assaulted Briggs' senses as he teetered on the edge of the open doorway, the vast expanse of sky and earth beckoning him. With a leap of faith, he threw himself into the abyss, his body hurtling through the air, torn between the realms of nightmare and reality.

As he descended, the nightmare began to fade, the crashing plane and the chaos receding into the recesses of his mind. The haunting memories of fallen comrades merged with the present reality, reminding Briggs of the sacrifices and unwavering determination to complete the mission.

The parachute deployed, Briggs felt a momentary suspension in time as he floated through the vastness of the sky. The world below him stretched out, a tapestry of challenges and uncertainties waiting to be faced. Amidst the serenity of the descent, his focus sharpened, his resolve fortified.

Briggs landed on the ground with a thud, his body jarred by the impact. But the pain was fleeting, overshadowed by the surge of adrenaline and the unwavering determination that coursed through his veins.

A sense of apprehension hung heavily in Alexander Q's office the next day. This time there was light in the room. The room was adorned with the trappings of power, its walls lined with bookshelves filled with volumes of knowledge and mementoes from past missions. The atmosphere was tense, and Briggs could sense that all was not well.

Alexander Q, sat behind a grand mahogany desk, his expression was stern and unyielding. His piercing gaze met Briggs' eyes, an unspoken disappointment across his features. The weight of his disapproval was palpable, casting a heavy cloud over the room.

"I expected better from you, Briggs.' Q began, his voice laced with a hint of disappointment.
'What happened in Durango's facility was nothing short of a debacle. Lives were lost, chaos ensued, and the mission objectives were compromised."

Briggs felt the weight of Q's words like a punch to the gut. He knew that his actions, or lack thereof, had consequences. The realization that lives had been lost, and the mission had faltered under his watch gnawed at his conscience.

Briggs stood there quiet

Q leaned back in his chair, his gaze unwavering. "Durango is a formidable adversary, I'll give you that," he said, his voice tinged with a mix of respect and frustration. "But it's your role as an agent to anticipate the unexpected, to adapt and overcome. And yet, it seems that you were blindsided by this plot, which compromised the mission and the lives of your fellow agents!"

Q's scolding grew more intense, his disappointment transforming into an unyielding anger. He did not wait for an explanation from Briggs, as he unleashed a barrage of criticism and reprimand. Each word felt like a blow to Briggs.

"You have become a liability, Briggs," Q's voice echoed through the room, its sharpness cutting through the air. "Your inability to anticipate Durango's plans and failure to protect your team have cost us dearly. Lives were lost, resources squandered, and our organization's reputation tarnished."

His failures settled heavily upon him, his shoulders sagging under the weight of Q's scathing remarks.

"You were once one of our best agents," Q continued, his tone laced with frustration and regret. "But it seems that time has caught up with you, Briggs. Perhaps you have grown complacent, and lost your edge. This mission was supposed to be a routine assignment, yet you allowed it to spiral into chaos."

Briggs' mind raced as he searched for words to defend himself, explain the mission's intricacies and the unforeseen betrayal that had unfolded. But before he could speak, Q's relentless tirade continued, leaving no room for justification.

"I have given you opportunities, Briggs," Q's voice dripped with disappointment. "Opportunities to prove your worth, to demonstrate that you can still carry out the missions entrusted to you. And yet, time and again, you have let us down."

As Q's scolding reached its crescendo, Briggs felt a mixture of regret, and determination to prove himself again. The fire within him, though dimmed by the onslaught of Q's disapproval, flickered with a faint glimmer of hope.

"I understand, sir," Briggs finally managed to speak, his voice laced with remorse and determination. "I take full responsibility for the failures of the mission, and I acknowledge that I need to reassess my abilities and regain the trust that has been lost."

'No, Briggs. You won't have to worry about that ever again.' He reached for the intercom on his desk and pressed a button, summoning Christopher. Christopher's arrival was swift, his footsteps echoing in the tense silence.

"Christopher, step forward," Q commanded, his voice firm but tinged with regret. Christopher, his face etched with confusion and concern, complied, standing beside Briggs, who wore a mix of resignation and disbelief.

Q fixed his gaze on Christopher, his eyes betraying admiration and resolve. "Christopher," he began, his voice steady, "in light of recent events and the need for a fresh perspective, I have decided to assign you as the lead on this case. You possess the necessary skills, experience, and tenacity to tackle the challenges ahead."

Christopher's brows furrowed, his shock palpable. He glanced at Briggs, silently searching for answers, but found only a mirror of his astonishment. This sudden turn of events had caught them both off guard.

"But sir, Briggs and I have always been a team," Christopher interjected, his voice laced with concern. "We have faced countless missions together, and our combined expertise has always yielded successful results. Is this truly necessary?"

Q's gaze hardened, "I appreciate the bond and camaraderie you share with Briggs," he replied firmly, almost snapping. "However, given recent circumstances, fresh perspectives are required to ensure success. You will have the agency's full support, and I will provide any assistance you require in a different capacity."

Christopher's mind raced, torn between his loyalty to Briggs and his commitment to the agency. He understood the weight of Q's decision, recognizing that it was made in the mission's best interest and their team's safety. Yet, the suddenness of the announcement left him grappling with a mixture of emotions.

"Sir...," Christopher stammered, his voice betraying confusion and concern. Christopher wanted to say, 'I value Briggs' expertise and trust him implicitly. How will this affect our dynamic as a team?" but he dared not see Alexander wasn't in the best mood.

At that moment, Christopher and Briggs stood silent, their expressions a mix of shock and resignation. Q's reputation as a highly respected figure within the agency left no room for questioning his decisions. They understood the weight of his authority and knew that challenging his judgment would only lead to further repercussions.

Christopher's hand slowly retreated, and he exchanged a brief glance with Briggs, their unspoken connection conveying a mixture of disappointment and determination. They both realized their loyalty to the agency surpassed their desires and ambitions. It was a testament to their professionalism and commitment to the greater mission.

Though shaken by the sudden events, Briggs managed to find a sense of acceptance within himself. He knew Q's decision was made with the best intentions, even if it meant a temporary setback for him.

As Christopher and Briggs stepped out of Q's office, the weight of the situation settled upon them. The news of their separation, the abrupt shift in their roles, left Briggs deeply unsettled. While he was accustomed to navigating the shadows and murky waters of the intelligence world, he knew that Christopher had a different nature—and unwavering purity that often shone through his actions.

Briggs couldn't help but worry for his partner. Christopher's kind heart and compassionate nature had always been both a strength and a vulnerability. It made him an exceptional agent, able to connect with people on a deeper level, but it also left him susceptible to the darker side of the job.

As they walked down the corridor, Briggs glanced sideways at Christopher, his concern evident in his eyes. "Christopher," he began, his voice laced with worry and caution. "This case, it's not like anything we've encountered before. The darkness within it runs deep, and I fear it may test your resolve."

Christopher met Briggs' gaze, his expression a mix of determination and understanding. "I know, Briggs," he replied, his voice steady. "I'm well aware of the dangers that lie ahead. But I also believe that light can prevail, even in the darkest times. We've faced adversity before, and we've come out stronger. This will be no different."

Briggs admired Christopher's unwavering optimism, his ability to find hope in the face of despair. Yet, he couldn't help but worry that this particular case might prove to be a formidable challenge—one that even Christopher's indomitable spirit might struggle to overcome.

"Christopher, I've seen things in this line of work that can break a person," Briggs cautioned, his voice tinged with a lifetime of experience. "Evil exists, and it takes many forms. It preys on the innocent, manipulates the vulnerable."

Christopher's face contorted with a mix of determination and vulnerability. "Briggs, I appreciate your worry, but I refuse to let fear dictate my actions," he asserted. "I will hold onto my belief in justice and use it as a shield against the darkness."

Briggs sighed, realizing the futility of trying to dissuade Christopher from his unwavering optimism. He respected his partner's resolve, even if he couldn't fully comprehend it. Perhaps Christopher's pure-heartedness had kept them grounded throughout their years of service, providing a beacon of light in a world often consumed by shadows.

"Very well, Christopher," Briggs conceded, a mix of resignation and reluctant admiration in his voice. "I won't stand in the way of your convictions. Just promise me one thing: you'll remain vigilant and not let your guard down. The darkness we face can be relentless, and it takes more than just a pure heart to withstand its onslaught."

Christopher nodded. "I promise, Briggs," he said, his voice resolute.

As they continued down the corridor, their footsteps echoing in the silence, Briggs couldn't shake off his worries entirely. But he also knew that Christopher possessed a strength beyond his purity of heart—a resilience and determination forged through their shared experiences.

Briggs made his way to Racheal's place. He walked in and stood at the doorway, silently observing Racheal as she did her household chores. Briggs stood silently at the doorway, his eyes fixed on Racheal as she moved about the room. The soft rays of sunlight filtered through the windows, casting a warm glow on her figure. She wore an oversized red t-shirt that accentuated her delicate features, and her hair was casually pulled back into a loose ponytail, strands of hair framing her face.

As Racheal sorted through the laundry, her movements were graceful and effortless. She hummed a soft melody, lost in her own world of domestic tasks. Briggs found himself captivated by her beauty in that simple moment. There was a certain allure to her casual attire and the relaxed way she did her chores.

The red t-shirt clung gently to Racheal's curves, emphasizing her feminine form. It was a vibrant colour that complemented her complexion, making her look even more radiant. The fabric accentuated her every movement, creating an air of casual elegance. Briggs couldn't help but be drawn to her magnetic presence.

Her ponytail, loosely gathered at the nape of her neck, revealed the graceful curve of her slender neck. Stray wisps of hair framed her face, giving her a slightly dishevelled yet alluring appearance. There was an effortless charm in how she carried herself as if she were at ease in her skin.

Briggs silently moved closer, his footsteps muffled by the softness of the carpet. He watched Racheal's focused expression as she folded a freshly washed shirt. The scent of detergent lingered in the air, mingling with the faint fragrance of her perfume. It was a comforting aroma that spoke of home and familiarity.

Racheal was unaware of Briggs' presence, lost in her thoughts as she did her tasks. Her movements were graceful and precise, her hands gentle yet efficient. Briggs admired her dedication and attention to detail, finding solace in the ordinary moments they shared together.

The warm sunlight played across Racheal's features, accentuating her natural beauty. Her eyes sparkled with a hint of joy, and a soft smile graced her lips. There was a radiance about her that transcended any material adornment. It was the inner glow of contentment and love.

Briggs felt a sense of calm wash over him as he observed Racheal in her element. The worries and uncertainties that burdened his mind seemed to momentarily fade away. At that moment, all that mattered was the connection and comfort of their shared space.

He longed to reach out and touch her, to let her know he was there, but he hesitated, savouring the quiet beauty of the scene before him. He cherished this glimpse into her world of simple domesticity and unconditional love.

Racheal turned around, her eyes widening in surprise as she noticed Briggs standing there. A mix of emotions flickered across her face — surprise, joy, and a hint of apprehension. Briggs moved closer, closing the distance between them, gently brushing a loose strand of hair behind her ear.

"You're a sight for sore eyes," Briggs whispered, his voice filled with affection and longing. Racheal's gaze met his, and he saw a range of emotions in her eyes.

She reached out and gently cupped his face with her palm, her touch tender and filled with affection. Her fingers grazed over the wounds on his face, and Briggs couldn't help but lean into her touch, savouring the comfort it brought. It was a silent exchange of love, an unspoken understanding passing between them.

Briggs closed his eyes, relishing the sensation of Racheal's touch against his skin. He felt a surge of gratitude for her presence in his life, for the strength and solace she provided. At that moment, he wanted to ensure that this was real, that he wasn't merely lost in a dream or illusion.

He kissed her palm softly, his lips lingering there briefly. The gesture was his way of confirming the reality of their reunion, a reassurance that Racheal was indeed there by his side. It was an affirmation of his love and commitment to her.

A single tear escaped Racheal's eye, tracing a path down her cheek. She whispered softly, her voice filled with emotions, "You came back." Her words held both relief and a touch of vulnerability. Briggs nodded, his eyes glistening with unshed tears, unable to find words to express the depth of his emotions.

Silence enveloped them, and for a moment, time stood still. They didn't need words to communicate; their connection ran more profound than mere conversations. It was a bond forged through shared experiences, laughter, and tears.

Racheal pulled him close and embraced him. In that embrace, the weight of their shared experiences seemed to dissipate. Briggs could feel the tension and exhaustion melt away, replaced by a sense of peace and belonging. It was a moment of pure connection, a refuge from the chaos and uncertainty surrounding them.

They held each other tightly, their bodies intertwined, finding solace in the warmth of their embrace. The world outside faded into insignificance as they clung to one another, cherishing the precious moments of togetherness. They found strength, love, and a renewed sense of purpose in that intimate space.

For Briggs, this was a turning point, a realization that the battles they faced were not worth sacrificing the love and stability they had built together. Racheal's touch, acceptance, and unwavering support reaffirmed his decision to prioritize their relationship over the dangerous pursuits that had consumed him.

In that tender embrace, Briggs knew that he had found his sanctuary in Racheal's arms. He vowed to protect her, to cherish their love,

Briggs stood in Racheal's apartment, his heart racing with mixed emotions. The room was filled with a soft, warm glow as sunlight filtered through the curtains, casting gentle shadows on the walls. Wearing a simple yet captivating red dress, Racheal stood before him, her eyes reflecting a blend of surprise and delight.

Unable to longer contain his longing, Briggs reached out and gently cupped Racheal's face. Her skin felt soft and warm against his touch, sending a shiver of anticipation through his body. She leaned into his hand, her eyes searching his as if seeking reassurance and confirmation that this moment was real.

Their embrace deepened as they wrapped their arms around each other, drawing closer every second. Their bodies pressed against each other like they were made for one another. Briggs could feel Racheal's heartbeat against his chest, a rhythmic melody synchronising with his own.

As they held each other, time seemed to slow down, allowing them to savour the tenderness of their connection. They revelled in the sensations, the gentle brush of their lips against each other's skin, the warmth of their breath mingling in the air. The world outside ceased to exist as they became enveloped in their private sanctuary.

The intensity between them grew with each touch, each caress, fueling a fiery desire that had long been smouldering within their souls. Their kisses deepened, filled with a passionate hunger that could no longer be contained. It was as if their years apart had only fueled the fire of their love, making this reunion even more intense and profound.

Briggs savoured the taste of Racheal's lips, their sweetness a balm to his weary soul. He ran his fingers through her hair, feeling the soft strands slip through his fingertips. Racheal's hands explored his back, tracing invisible patterns across his skin, leaving a trail of longing in their wake.

They moved as if in a dance, their bodies swaying in perfect harmony, utterly attuned to each other's desires. The world outside ceased to exist, their surroundings fading into the background as they surrendered to the intoxicating bliss of their connection.

Time seemed to lose its meaning as they lost themselves in each other. Their passion ignited like wildfire, consuming them with a fierce and insatiable hunger. Their breaths became ragged, their bodies entwined in a symphony of desire.

As their bodies intermingled, their sweats mingling, and their hearts beating in unison, they created a haven where time stood still. They lay on the bed, naked, flesh to flesh, soul to soul.

In the warmth of each other's arms, they discovered a renewed sense of hope and a profound understanding that no matter what challenges lay ahead, they could face them together. They were united by a love that had withstood the test of time, a love that could conquer any obstacle in its path.

As the afternoon sun continued its journey across the sky, casting its golden glow upon them, Briggs and Racheal remained locked in their embrace, knowing that this moment was precious and fleeting.

CHAPTER SEVEN

Christopher walked into the cemetery with a white lotus cradled gently in his hands. It was a serene and solemn place, filled with rows of gravestones and a sense of stillness that seemed to hang in the air. As he walked through the paths, he felt sorrow and nostalgia enveloping his heart.

The trees stood tall, branches reaching the sky, casting a dapple shade over the landscape. The soft whisper of the wind rustled through the leaves, creating a gentle symphony that echoed through the cemetery.

He approached a familiar gravestone marked 'Alicesa', his mother's name. The simple yet elegant stone stood as a tribute to her life. Christopher knelt down and carefully placed the white lotus on the ground.

As he stood there, surrounded by the hushed silence of the cemetery, memories of his mother flooded his mind. He recalled her loving presence, the way she held his hand as they walked together, her voice soothing and comforting. She had been his anchor, a constant source of support and guidance.

Christopher reminisced about the mornings when his mother would drive him to school, her smile radiating warmth as they embarked on their daily routine. He could almost hear her laughter and eyes filled with pride and love. She had always been there to protect and keep him safe in a world that often seemed unpredictable and harsh.

The cemetery seemed to embrace Christopher, offering him a space to reflect and find solace in his memories. He closed his eyes and allowed the stillness to envelop him as if his mother's presence lingered in the air. He almost felt her gentle touch as if she was reaching him from beyond the veil.

In the quietude of the cemetery, Christopher found himself whispering words of gratitude and love to his mother. He thanked her for the countless sacrifices she had made and for the unwavering love she had bestowed upon him. He longed to hear her voice again, to seek her guidance in the intricate complexities of life.

As Christopher stood there, surrounded by nature's beauty and his mother's memory, he realized their bond transcended the physical realm. Even though she was no longer with him in a tangible sense, her love nourished his spirit, providing him with strength and resilience.

With a heavy heart, Christopher recalled the memory of his mother's tragic departure. He closed his eyes and allowed the memories to flood his mind, as painful as they were. The image of his mother, a dedicated police officer, filled his thoughts.

He remembered the day when his mother set out on a mission to apprehend a notorious drug lord. She relentlessly pursued justice, determined to make the streets safer for her community.

Christopher admired her courage and unwavering commitment to her duty.

But tragedy struck during her mission. As she closed in on the drug lord, one of his men turned against her. Three gunshots pierced the air in a moment of betrayal, forever changing Christopher's life. It was a moment etched into his memory, filled with shock and disbelief.

Christopher's mother, a pillar of strength and resilience, fell victim to the forces she had dedicated her life to combat. The loss was personal and a blow to the community she had served selflessly. Her absence left a void that could never be filled.

As Christopher stood in the cemetery, he couldn't help but feel a mixture of anger, grief, and a burning desire for justice. The pain of her loss was still fresh, and the wounds in his heart had yet to fully heal.

But amidst the sorrow, Christopher also found solace in the memories of his mother's unwavering spirit. She had been a beacon of light, shining brightly in the face of darkness. Her determination and sacrifice had left an indelible mark on his soul, inspiring him to continue her legacy of fighting for what was right.

As Christopher stood in the cemetery, he thought of Briggs at that moment. He had always relied on his partner's experience and guidance, and now he faced the unknown without him. The weight of the responsibility settled heavily on his shoulders, and he contemplated his next steps.

As he gazed at the rows of tombstones, Christopher knew he couldn't let despair take hold of him. He had been trained to be resilient, to adapt to challenging situations, and to find strength in adversity. Briggs had instilled in him a sense of determination and the belief that they could make a difference together, but it was up to Christopher to carry on their mission.

He couldn't help but think back to the briefing from Q, where he had learned about the true nature of the terrorist cell they were up against.

Thomas had provided crucial information during his interrogation, shedding light on the composition and motivations of the group.

Thomas said the cell consisted of former FBI, CIA, and SIS agents and Russian operatives. These individuals had all felt betrayed by the systems they once served, harbouring deep resentment and anger towards the establishments that had once been their homes. This shared sense of betrayal had brought them together, forging an unlikely alliance that aimed to dismantle the very systems they had once sworn to protect.

As Christopher absorbed this information, he couldn't help but feel anger, frustration, and determination. The realization that the enemy they were facing was not just a collection of faceless terrorists but somewhat disillusioned and vengeful former agents added another layer of complexity to the already intricate web of their mission.

Deep down, Christopher understood the depths of their anger and frustration. With all its flaws and bureaucracy, the system had failed these individuals somehow, leading them down a path of disillusionment. However, he also knew their methods were misguided, resorting to violence and destruction to bring about change. Christopher believed in upholding the law, seeking justice through legal means, and protecting innocent lives.

Christopher stood in the dimly lit room, facing Thomas. It was a tense atmosphere, charged with the weight of secrets and the urgency of the mission. Q, the stern and unwavering figure of authority, sat across from him, his piercing gaze fixed on Thomas.

As the interrogation continued, Q wasted no time cutting to the chase. He demanded answers, wanting to know the extent of the terrorist cell's plans and the agencies involved. Thomas, however, remained defiant, his eyes filled with a mix of fear and determination.

Thomas spoke with conviction, his voice steady despite the perilous situation. He explained that their ultimate goal was not just to tear down the system they felt had failed them, but to establish a new order—a particular order that would rise from the ashes of the old. It was a chilling revelation, highlighting the dangerous ideology that fueled the actions of the terrorist cell.

Q pressed Thomas to reveal the agencies already involved, but the double agent refused to comply. He spoke of an unyielding loyalty, claiming that even the fear of death was not enough to make him betray his comrades. His resolve seemed unshakeable as if he had accepted the consequences of his actions long before this moment.

Frustration filled the room as Q grew more relentless in his pursuit of the truth. He promised Thomas that if he remained silent, a fate worse than death awaited him. The threat hung heavy in the air, but Thomas refused to yield. It was a dangerous game of cat and mouse, with higher stakes than anyone could have imagined.

As the interrogation progressed, Christopher observed the exchange, his mind racing with the weight of the situation.

Q's relentless questioning continued, but Thomas remained steadfast, his loyalty to the cause unyielding. The tension in the room reached its peak, the air thick with anticipation. Christopher knew they had to find a breakthrough, a crack in Thomas' armour that would lead them closer to the truth.

Suddenly, Q rose from his seat, his presence dominating the room. His voice dripped with a steely determination. He stared directly into Thomas' eyes, revealing a deep resolve that sent shivers down Christopher's spine.

Q spoke with chilling certainty, painting a vivid picture of the consequences Thomas would face if he didn't cooperate; life stripped of purpose, a shadow existence where Thomas would be haunted by the knowledge of the destruction he had wrought. It was a fate that surpassed physical pain; it was a punishment that would torment his soul.

The room fell into an eerie silence as Q's words echoed in the air. Christopher watched as Thomas's face contorted with fear and doubt. For a moment, it seemed as though the double agent's unwavering loyalty wavered as if the weight of his actions bore down upon him.

But then, just as quickly, Thomas regained his composure. He locked eyes with Q, defiance burning in his gaze. He was prepared to face whatever fate awaited him, unwilling to compromise the cause he believed in. It was heartbreaking to see someone so deeply entrenched in their convictions that they were willing to sacrifice everything.

As the interrogation concluded, Q sighed with frustration and disappointment. It was clear that Thomas would not break, that the truth they sought would remain buried for now.

Christopher walked out of the cemetery and walked to his car. He sat in his car, his hands gripping the steering wheel tightly as he navigated the bustling city streets. The weight of the recent revelations and the danger that loomed over him weighed heavily on his mind. At that moment, the thoughts of Bretty flooded his consciousness, and he couldn't shake the worry that gnawed at his core.

As he drove, memories of their time together flickered through his mind like an old film reel. Bretty, with her infectious laughter and fierce determination, had become an integral part of his life. They had faced danger side by side. But now, with the shadow of Durango hanging over them, everything had changed.

Christopher's thoughts drifted back to the moment he had last seen Bretty. They had been together, working tirelessly to unravel the twisted web of the terrorist cell's plans. But as chaos erupted and bullets filled the air, they were forced to split up. Christopher had lost sight of

Bretty in the ensuing mayhem, and worry gnawed at his heart like a relentless predator.

The possibility that Bretty had fallen into Durango's clutches haunted him. Durango's sinister nature and organization sent shivers down Christopher's spine. He knew firsthand the brutality they were capable of, and witnessed the depths of their darkness. The thought of Bretty in their clutches filled him with a desperate need to find her, to ensure her safety.

Christopher's mind raced with different scenarios as he manoeuvred through the traffic. He wondered if Bretty had managed to escape and was hiding, waiting for the right moment to regroup. Or perhaps she had been captured, forced to endure unimaginable hardships at the hands of Durango and his men. The mere thought of her suffering fueled his determination to find her.

His hands gripped the steering wheel tighter, his knuckles turning white. He couldn't let fear paralyze him, couldn't succumb to the overwhelming weight of the situation.

As Christopher continued his drive, he felt a renewed determination coursing through his veins. He knew he couldn't afford to dwell on the worst-case scenarios. Instead, he focused on the strength and resilience that defined Bretty. He had seen her face countless challenges head-on, her unwavering spirit a beacon of light in even the darkest times.

Christopher entered his apartment, closing the door behind him. The space greeted him with a sense of familiarity and solace, a refuge from the chaos of the outside world. The apartment, bathed in warm, soft lighting, emanated a calm ambience that instantly eased his troubled mind.

The living room exuded a sense of order and simplicity with its minimalist design. The sleek and understated furniture blended seamlessly with the neutral colour palette of the walls. A comfortable sofa stood against one wall, inviting him to sink into its plush cushions and find respite from the relentless pursuit of the truth.

The large board dominating one corner of the room caught Christopher's attention. The board, mounted on the wall, was a mosaic of investigation—a visual representation of his relentless pursuit of justice. The surface was covered with photographs, newspaper clippings, and handwritten notes, all meticulously organized to reveal the interconnected web of his targets.

Each picture represented a puzzle piece, a person of interest in his ongoing investigations. Christopher's focused determination was evident in how he pinned the images, ensuring that no detail went unnoticed. The faces stared back at him, captured in freeze-frame moments, their eyes filled with secrets waiting to be unravelled.

Thin threads stretched between the photographs, forming a delicate tapestry of connections and leads. The threads represented the links Christopher had discovered, the trails he had followed, and the paths leading him closer to the truth. It was a visual representation of his relentless pursuit, a physical manifestation of his commitment to solving the mysteries that plagued his mind.

Christopher approached the board, his fingers tracing the threads delicately as he absorbed the information displayed before him. The board was a constant reminder of the weight of his responsibilities, the lives at stake and the justice that needed to be served. It was a tangible symbol of his dedication, a focal point that anchored him amidst the chaos of his investigations.

His targets' faces stared back at him, their eyes seeming to hold both defiance and fear. He had spent countless hours examining their histories, connections, and crimes. Each detail, each piece of evidence, was a step closer to unravelling the truth.

Around the board, shelves held an array of reference materials—books on criminal psychology, forensics, and intelligence analysis.

Christopher was a student of his craft, constantly expanding his knowledge and sharpening his skills. The shelves also housed various mementoes from past cases—a bullet casing, a worn-out surveillance device, and a small statue of justice, its scales forever balanced.

Christopher walked over to the refrigerator, the cool air washing over him as he opened the door. He reached for a chilled beer, the refreshing beverage a temporary respite from the intensity of his investigations. With the bottle in hand, he took a long sip, savouring the familiar taste that provided a momentary escape.

His mind focused on his next move as he paced before the investigation board. He knew that to thwart Durango's plans and prevent the devastation from reaching American soil, he needed to forge alliances with agents on the other side of the Atlantic. Collaboration and coordination were essential to ensure success.

His fingers traced the threads on the board, his eyes scanning the faces and names representing the individuals involved. Christopher contemplated the potential contacts he could contact, agents who shared his determination and were equally committed to dismantling the terrorist cell. He mentally composed a list of potential allies, their expertise and resources forming a powerful force against Durango's nefarious intentions.

While his primary objective was to halt Durango's plans, another pressing matter weighed on his mind. He felt needed to speak with Briggs to uncover the information Durango had disclosed when they had ambushed his men. Christopher knew that Briggs held a crucial piece of the puzzle that could propel their investigation forward and shed light on the terrorist cell's inner workings.

Setting down his beer momentarily, Christopher reached for his phone and dialled Briggs' number. Mid-way to its ringing, Christopher cut the call perhaps Briggs needed this break from the case, he thought. He knew how much Briggs would love to spend these moments alone with Racheal undisturbed.

Christopher returned to pacing the room, his mind abuzz with the possibilities ahead. Christopher's hands instinctively ran through his hair as he continued to pace. He envisioned different scenarios, mapping out his paths, anticipating the challenges and obstacles that awaited him.

With each step and sip, Christopher felt a renewed sense of purpose coursing through his veins. The determination in his eyes reflected the unwavering resolve that had propelled him this far. He knew the road ahead would be treacherous, fraught with danger and uncertainty, but he was prepared to face it head-on.

As the last sip of beer disappeared, Christopher set the bottle aside and returned his focus to the investigation board. He adjusted the threads, connecting the puzzle pieces more intricately, as if drawing a map of the battles ahead. The information gathered, the clues deciphered, and the contacts to be made converged into a plan of action.

Christopher's heart skipped a beat as he heard the knock on the door. He talked to the door and open it, his mind bracing for any possibility. Standing at his doorstep was Bretty, her face covered in blood, her once-lustrous hair in disarray, and her clothes torn and battered. Shock coursed through Christopher's veins as he instinctively reached out to catch her falling form.

Without hesitation, Christopher swept Bretty into his arms, feeling the weight of her limp body against his chest. The scent of blood mingled with the air, intensifying his concern for her well-being. He carried her inside, carefully closing the door behind him, and gently laid her on the couch.

Christopher's hands trembled with worry and urgency as he assessed her injuries. Her temple was stained crimson, the blood matted in her hair. His heart raced as he realized the severity of the situation. With swift movements, he fetched a damp cloth from the kitchen and gently cleaned the blood from her face, taking care not to cause any further harm.

His mind raced, trying to comprehend what had happened to Bretty. Who could have attacked her so mercilessly? The connection between Durango's reach and Bretty's involvement in the case became seemingly clear. It appeared that the threat had extended far beyond Christopher and Briggs.

As Christopher tended to Bretty's injuries, his thoughts were consumed by fear and determination. He vowed to protect her at all costs, to bring those responsible for her suffering to justice.

Once he had tended to her wounds as best he could, Christopher fetched a soft blanket from his bedroom and draped it over her, ensuring she was warm and comfortable. He sat by her side, watching over her as she lay there, her breathing steady and serene despite her ordeal.

As the hours ticked by, Christopher remained steadfast by Bretty's side, his gaze fixed upon her face. The flickering light of a nearby lamp cast a warm glow, accentuating the contours of her delicate features. At that moment, his desire to protect her grew stronger.

Bretty's eyelids fluttered open, revealing tired but grateful eyes. She mustered a weak smile as her gaze met Christopher's concerned expression. Slowly, she propped herself up on the couch, supported by a few soft cushions.

Christopher gently admonished her, his voice filled with worry and relief, "What happened, Bretty? Your injuries could be serious. Why didn't you go to the hospital first?"

Bretty nodded weakly, understanding his concern. "I know, Christopher, but I couldn't risk going to a hospital. Durango's men were after me. They captured me and handed me over to Tony. He locked me up and... and punished me."

A mix of anger and concern rose within Christopher as he listened to Bretty's harrowing account. Taking a deep breath, he composed himself and gently grasped Bretty's hand.

"I'm glad you managed to escape, Bretty," Christopher said softly, his voice filled with sincerity. "You did the right thing by coming here. You're safe now."

Bretty nodded, her eyes reflecting a blend of relief and exhaustion. "I knew I could trust you, Christopher. I knew this was the safest place for me to seek refuge."

Bretty leaned back against the cushions, her body still weak and battered. She recounted the horrors she had endured, the fear that had consumed her as she fought for her freedom. Christopher listened intently, his expression a mix of empathy and determination.

After Bretty had finished sharing her ordeal, Christopher rose from his seat, his resolve firm and unwavering. "You need to rest now. I'll ensure you're safe, and that justice is served."

Bretty nodded, gratitude shining in her eyes.

As she settled back into the couch, Christopher tucked a soft blanket around her, ensuring she was comfortable and warm. He lingered for a moment, his gaze lingering on her face, etching her image into his mind as a reminder of why he fought so tirelessly against the forces of darkness.

Christopher retreated to his study. He closed the door, seeking solace in the confines of his room. Conflicting emotions churned within him, causing a knot in his stomach. He had been deeply concerned for Bretty's welfare, but now that he had seen her, something felt amiss, a nagging sense of unease that he couldn't shake.

Sitting on the edge of his bed, Christopher ran a hand through his tousled hair, his brow furrowed with worry. He replayed the encounter with Bretty in his mind, trying to pinpoint the source of his uneasiness. She had appeared weak and vulnerable, her injuries telling a tale of the horrors she had endured. Yet, something about her demeanour and how she recounted her escape didn't quite add up.

He reached for his phone, his fingers hovering over the screen as he contemplated calling Briggs. He needed a sounding board, someone to share his concerns with. But then doubt crept in, and he hesitated. Briggs had been through a lot, and Christopher couldn't bear further burdening him with his suspicions. Maybe it was best to keep his thoughts to himself, for now, to gather more evidence before drawing any conclusions.

With a sigh, Christopher set his phone aside, realizing he was alone in this investigation. He knew he had to trust his instincts and tread cautiously. The stakes were higher than ever, and he couldn't afford to make any missteps.

The room was quiet, and the weight of the situation settled heavily upon Christopher's shoulders. He stared out the window, watching the night sky, seeking solace in the distant stars. The city's hustle and bustle faded away, leaving him alone with his thoughts.

In the quiet solitude of the evening, Christopher and Bretty sat at the dining table, their plates filled with a comforting meal. The room was bathed in a warm, soft glow, casting gentle shadows that danced upon the walls. An air of uncertainty lingered between them, prompting Christopher to break the silence.

"Bretty, may I ask you something?" Christopher's voice was gentle, his eyes locked with hers. "I couldn't help but notice your accent. It's not quite British. Where are you originally from?"

Bretty paused momentarily, her gaze flickering as memories stirred within her. She took a deep breath before responding, her voice hinting melancholy. "I know that I was born in Argentina. But my parents... they died before I had the chance to meet them. I know they were immigrants, but I don't know where they were from."

Christopher nodded, his curiosity mingled with empathy. He could sense the longing in Bretty's words, the yearning to connect with her roots, to unravel the mysteries of her own identity. He understood that feeling all too well, having grappled with his own past.

"I'm sorry for bringing up such a sensitive topic, Bretty," Christopher said softly. "I didn't mean to intrude."

Bretty offered a small smile, her eyes shimmering with gratitude and sadness. "It's alright, Christopher. It's a part of my story, even if it's uncertain. Maybe someday I'll find out more about where I'm from."

Christopher's heart was filled with empathy for Bretty's loss as they continued eating. He felt the need to share a part of his own story, to let her know that she wasn't alone in her pain.

"I want you to know that I understand the pain of losing someone you love," Christopher began, "My mother... she was an incredible person. Kind, compassionate, and full of life. But she was taken from us too soon."

Bretty's eyes widened, her gaze locked on Christopher as she listened intently...

"She was a cop caught in the crossfire of a senseless act of violence," Christopher continued, his voice quivering slightly. "A gunman... he fired three bullets into her heart. It was a tragedy that shattered our lives."

Bretty gently placed her hand on Christopher's, offering comfort in the face of his pain. Her eyes conveyed a deep understanding, as if she could feel the weight of his loss.

With a bittersweet smile, he continued, "But amidst the heartbreak, I hold on to the beautiful memories we shared. The moments that remind me of her warmth and love. She taught me to fight for justice, to stand up against those who bring harm to others."

Christopher's voice grew stronger as he spoke, filled with determination born from his mother's legacy. He recounted stories of her selflessness, her unwavering dedication to making a difference in the world.

In the silence that followed, Christopher reached for Bretty's hand, holding it tightly. Their shared experiences had created a bond, a connection that transcended words. They understood the depth of loss and the determination to make a difference in a world plagued by darkness.

In that moment, they found solace in each other's presence, drawing strength from the shared pain and purpose that bound them together.

As Christopher shared his heartfelt story, Bretty instinctively reached out to him. Her delicate hands gently cradled his face, her touch warm and comforting. Their connection grew stronger, and Christopher couldn't help but be captivated by her presence.

Bretty's face, illuminated by the room's soft glow, revealed striking and alluring features. Her chiseled face showcased high cheekbones that added an air of elegance to her overall appearance. Full and undeniably enticing, her lips carried a hint of a smile that hinted at a playful nature.

But her eyes held Christopher's attention, drawing him in with their mesmerizing hue. They were like sapphires, bright and sparkling. The depth and intensity within her gaze revealed a wisdom and compassion that went beyond her years. In those blue orbs, he saw a reflection of his own desires and hopes.

Her nose, delicate and button-like, accentuated the harmony of her facial features, adding a touch of innocence to her captivating allure. Her perfectly proportioned features and a subtle radiance from within created a magnetic aura around her.

As their eyes met, a palpable connection sparked between them. In that instant, time seemed to stand still as they locked gazes, each seeing a reflection of their own desires and vulnerabilities in the other. The intensity of their shared gaze conveyed an unspoken understanding, a mutual longing that transcended words.

Desire flickered in Bretty's eyes as she leaned in closer, her breath mingling with Christopher's. The air crackled with anticipation, the unspoken tension between them growing more potent by the second. They could feel their hearts beating in unison, drawn to the magnetic pull of their shared emotions.

Overcome by the moment's intensity, Christopher reciprocated Bretty's gaze with equal fervour. His eyes mirrored his longing, a mixture of desire, vulnerability, and a yearning for connection. It was as if the weight of their shared pain and the understanding they had found in each other had forged a bond that surpassed the physical realm.

As Christopher and Bretty drew closer, an undeniable magnetism guided their movements. The air around them crackled with anticipation, their hearts beating in unison as they closed the physical distance between them.

With a gentle movement, Christopher shifted closer, their bodies inching toward each other on the cushioned surface of the dining table. The warmth emanating from their intertwined forms provided a respite from the chill of the evening that lingered beyond the confines of Christopher's room. The world outside seemed to disappear as they surrendered themselves to the moment.

Their eyes met again, conveying desire, vulnerability, and a shared understanding.

Bretty's fingers delicately traced the contours of Christopher's face, her touch feather-light and filled with an electric charge. Each caress spoke volumes, silently communicating a deep emotion that words could not express. The warmth of her touch seeped into his skin, igniting a fire within him that spread throughout his being.

With effortless grace, Christopher leaned closer, his breath mingling with Bretty's as they drew nearer. The space between them disappeared, replaced by an intoxicating intimacy that enveloped them both. The scent of their mingled fragrances lingered in the air, a sweet and heady reminder of their closeness.

Their lips finally met, a gentle collision that spoke of longing and longing fulfilled. Their kiss held a profound depth, as if the weight of their shared experiences and unspoken desires were encapsulated within that single act.

Time seemed to stand still as they explored each other's mouths, their tongues intertwining in a sensuous rhythm. Each touch and embrace conveyed a raw intensity expressing their mutual hunger and longing. In that stolen moment, they sought solace in each other's embrace, finding respite from the world beyond their private sanctuary.

Their bodies moved in sync, a harmonious symphony of desire and pleasure. Fingers entwined, hands explored, and clothing fell away, revealing the vulnerable beauty of their intertwined bodies. They revelled in the electric currents that surged through their veins, surrendering completely to their shared passion's intoxicating pull.

As their bodies merged in a tangle of limbs and shared breath, the world outside ceased to exist. They were consumed by the intoxicating bliss of the present moment, their connection deepening with each whisper of delight and each fervent caress. Time seemed irrelevant as they explored the depths of their desires, seeking solace and fulfilment in each other's arms.

In the warmth of their entwined bodies, they found sanctuary from the cold realities that awaited them beyond their intimate sanctuary. Their connection became a haven, a refuge where the weight of their burdens momentarily lifted, replaced by the intoxicating elixir of pleasure and connection.

With each gasp and moan, they revelled in the symphony of their desire, their bodies entwined in a dance as old as time. They surrendered to the rhythm of their passions, guided by an unspoken understanding and a shared longing for connection and intimacy.

Christopher carried Bretty into his room, his steps filled with anticipation and desire. The room was dimly lit, casting a warm and intimate glow. The door closed behind them as they entered, shutting out the world and leaving them in their private sanctuary.

Bretty turned to Christopher, her eyes filled with longing and vulnerability. The soft light highlighted her chiselled face, accentuating her high cheekbones and full, alluring lips. Her deep blue eyes shimmered with a captivating glow, drawing Christopher closer with their magnetic pull. Her nose, petite and button-like, added to her enchanting features.

They moved towards each other, their bodies gravitating as if pulled by an irresistible force. Their hearts beat in sync, echoing the rhythm of their longing.

As they came together, their lips met again in a tender and passionate kiss. The electricity coursed through their bodies intensified, igniting a fire within them. Their embrace deepened, and their hands began to explore each other's contours, tracing the curves and contours that had captivated their hearts and minds.

The world outside ceased to exist as they lost themselves in the depths of their connection. Their bodies intertwined, moving in harmony as they surrendered to the intoxicating dance of intimacy. Whispers of pleasure and sighs of ecstasy filled the room, intermingling with their shared breaths.

Time became irrelevant as their desires melded, each touch and caress building upon the intensity of their union. They revelled in the sensations that consumed them, their bodies moving with an instinctual rhythm, fueled by their love and longing.

The evening unfolded like a symphony of passion and tenderness, their bodies entwined in a sacred dance of intimacy. They explored the depths of each other's souls, discovering new realms of pleasure and connection. Their moans and gasps filled the room, harmonizing with the symphony of their love.

As the night wore on, their bodies intertwined in a tender embrace, finding solace and comfort in each other's arms. The world outside faded away, leaving only the two connected profoundly. They found solace, joy, and a sense of completeness.

The evening ended on a note of fulfilment and contentment, their bodies entangled in a warm and comforting embrace. They lay together, basking in the afterglow of their shared passion, their hearts and souls entwined.

In that private sanctuary of Christopher's room, they had created a sacred space where their love and desires merged. It was a moment to cherish, a memory to be etched in their hearts forever. They drifted off to sleep, wrapped in each other's arms.

The next day, Christopher awoke to remain in Bretty's warm embrace. As he opened his eyes, he saw that she was already awake, her eyes filled with worry and urgency. She moved gently, trying not to disturb him, as she prepared to leave.

Confusion clouded Christopher's mind as he watched Bretty quietly getting dressed. He couldn't help but notice the apprehension in her movements, as if she was in a hurry or trying to escape from something.

"What's going on? Why are you in such a rush?" he inquired, his voice tinged with concern.

Bretty paused momentarily, her gaze fixated on the window, her eyes scanning the surroundings as if she was on high alert. Her response came in a hushed and hurried tone, revealing her unease. "Christopher, I... I can't stay. It's not safe. I have to go."

The sudden change in her demeanour left him with worry in his stomach. He couldn't bear the thought of her being in danger, but he couldn't fully comprehend the reasons behind her urgency.

"Wait, Bretty. Tell me what's going on. Is there something I should know?" Christopher asked, a mixture of confusion and concern etched on his face.

Bretty turned to face him, her eyes filled with fear and sadness. She hesitated momentarily, as if torn between confiding in him and protecting him from whatever threat she faced. Eventually, she spoke in a low, determined voice.

"Christopher, I can't explain everything right now. But I need you to trust me. I'm involved in something dangerous that could also put your life at risk. I never wanted it to happen, but I have to go. Please understand."

Her words hung heavy in the air, leaving Christopher with a whirlwind of emotions.

Confusion, concern, and a deep longing to protect her battled within him. He gently grasped her hand, hoping to convey his support and understanding.

'Tell me, Brett.'

As Bretty continued to hastily dress, Christopher noticed her trembling hands and the fear that clouded her eyes. He couldn't help but feel a rush of concern for her safety. Sensing his confusion and worry, she took a deep breath and mustered the courage to explain the threatening call she had received.

With a quivering voice, Bretty started, 'Tony has resurfaced with a vengeance. He called me, and this time, he means business. Tony plans to leave the country soon, demanding that I accompany him. If I refused, he said he would hunt me down and end my life.'

Tears welled up in Bretty's eyes as she spoke, her vulnerability palpable. She explained that Tony had an extensive network of loyal and dangerous men, ready to carry out his bidding. Paranoia consumed her, fearing Tony's henchmen could burst through the door at any moment, ready to drag her away.

"I can't put you in danger, Christopher," Bretty whispered, her voice choked with emotion. "Tony is ruthless, and I don't want anything to happen to you because of me. I have to leave, find a way to stay hidden until I figure out how to confront him or escape his grasp."

Christopher's heart sank as he took in the weight of Bretty's words. He understood her fear and the dire predicament she faced. The thought of her being at the mercy of such a dangerous man was unbearable to him. Yet, he couldn't help but feel a surge of determination to protect her, to ensure her safety no matter the cost.

"I can't believe Tony would go to such lengths," Christopher muttered, his voice filled with anger and worry.

Reaching out, Christopher gently cupped Bretty's face in his hands, his eyes filled with concern and resolve. "Bretty, I won't let you face this alone. We'll find a way to outsmart Tony and keep ourselves safe. Leaving won't guarantee your security, and I can't bear being separated."

"Christopher," Bretty began, her voice tinged with concern, "I appreciate your willingness to help me, but this situation is too dangerous. I don't want to divert your focus from the case or put you at risk. You must stay focused on Durango and getting to the bottom of this."

Christopher's gaze softened, his hand reaching out to gently grasp Bretty's trembling fingers. "Bretty, getting Tony is not just a detour—it's a crucial step in unravelling the larger puzzle. If we can capture him, we might be able to extract vital information that can help us expose the entire network of ex-agents and Russian operatives. It's an opportunity to gain a significant advantage."

He continued, steady and determined, "I understand your concerns, but I can't sit idly by while you face this danger alone. We're a team, and together we can overcome any obstacles. We've already proven our resilience and resourcefulness. With your knowledge and my skills, we can navigate through this treacherous path and emerge stronger."

Bretty gazed into Christopher's eyes, her fear mingling with a glimmer of hope.

After a moment of contemplation, Bretty nodded, her voice filled with determination. "Alright, Christopher. Let's do this together. We'll confront Tony, and gather whatever information we can."

Christopher's face broke into a relieved smile, his grip on Bretty's hand tightening. "I promise we will face this head-on and come out stronger."

Christopher released a deep breath, his mind racing with thoughts and possibilities. He knew that time was of the essence, and they couldn't afford to waste a single moment. As they both sat down, he pulled out a notebook and a pen, ready to map out their next moves.

For hours, they brainstormed, linking ideas and crafting a plan to outmanoeuvre Tony and ensure their safety. Christopher's apartment became a hub of strategizing, with the large board on the wall now filled with notes, threads connecting pieces of information, and pictures of Tony and his known associates.

Christopher navigated the London streets that evening. A soft drizzle began to fall from the darkened sky, casting a melancholic hue over the city. The raindrops danced in the evening air, creating a misty veil that cloaked the streets and transformed the bustling metropolis into a scene of subdued beauty.

The glow of the streetlights shimmered through the rain, casting a gentle halo on the wet pavement below. The reflections of neon signs and passing car headlights blended with the cascading droplets, creating a mesmerizing symphony of colours that danced across the slick surface.

As Christopher maneuvered through the winding roads, the rhythmic sound of rain tapping against the car's roof and windows became a comforting companion, filling the silence within the vehicle. The rain enveloped the city in its delicate embrace, washing away the grime and troubles of the day, leaving behind a sense of renewal.

Pedestrians hurried along the rain-soaked sidewalks, their steps muffled by the steady downpour. Some sought refuge under awnings or umbrellas, while others embraced the rain, their faces turned skyward, allowing the cool droplets to kiss their skin. The city's pace seemed to slow as if the rain urged its inhabitants to pause and take a moment to brood at the day's happenings.

As Christopher's car sliced through the rain-soaked streets, his mind was consumed by the mission ahead. The absence of his usual companions and the task's weight made his solitude all the more noticeable. He had become accustomed to relying on the support and guidance of his team, but this time, it was different. He was going in alone.

Like a constant companion, the rain seemed to heighten his senses, its rhythmic pattern on the car's roof as a backdrop to his thoughts. The droplets streaked across the windshield, distorting the view of the city beyond, much like the unknown variables that loomed in his path. Christopher's mind was focused on the plan he had devised with Bretty.

Bretty was to intercept Tony, delaying him long enough for Christopher to arrive and apprehend him. She had chosen a London tunnel for their encounter, where Christopher could swiftly and discreetly take Tony into custody.

As Christopher envisioned the plan unfolding, a sense of both anticipation and unease coursed through his veins. It was risky, but his determination to unravel the truth and dismantle the dangerous network drove him forward. He couldn't shake the nagging feeling that something unexpected could occur and that unforeseen circumstances could mean their well-laid plans could be upended.

The rain seemed to mirror Christopher's internal turmoil, intensifying in its downpour as if nature acknowledged the gravity of the situation. The droplets on the windshield became a metaphor for the obstacles he would face, each a challenge that demanded his unwavering focus and skill.

In the solitude of his car, Christopher's thoughts drifted to Bretty. She had shown strength and resilience, proving to be a valuable ally in this treacherous game. Their connection, born out of shared danger and an unspoken understanding, had brought them together, but it also made Christopher fiercely protective of her. He couldn't help but worry for her safety, even as he trusted her to execute their plan flawlessly.

The rain-soaked streets passed by in a blur as Christopher honed his concentration. His training kicked in, allowing him to block distractions and focus solely on the mission.

As he neared the designated tunnel, Christopher's heartbeat quickened, a mix of adrenaline and apprehension surging through his veins. He knew that time was of the essence, that the success of their plan hinged on precise timing and unwavering execution.

Now a torrential downpour, the rain seemed to match Christopher's determination. It drummed on the roof of the car, providing a steady rhythm that fueled his resolve. With each passing mile, his mind focused on the objective, shutting out the distractions and doubts that threatened to derail him.

As Christopher finally arrived at the tunnel, the rain continued to cascade around him, creating a surreal atmosphere. The darkness ahead seemed to swallow the headlights' feeble attempt to penetrate the gloom, adding an air of mystery and anticipation to the scene.

Exiting the car, Christopher took a deep breath, steeling himself for what lay ahead. He knew that his actions in the coming moments would shape the outcome of this operation. The weight of responsibility rested squarely on his shoulders, but he drew strength from the thought of Bretty waiting for him, playing her part in this dangerous game of deception.

As Christopher entered the eerie, dimly lit tunnel, the surroundings transformed into a labyrinth of shadows and mystery. The faint glow of the few flickering lights cast long, distorted shadows on the damp walls, giving the tunnel an unsettling ambience. The air was heavy with a sense of anticipation, mingling with the scent of dampness and earth.

Positioning himself in the shadows, Christopher took a moment to collect his thoughts. His mind wandered back to Briggs, his trusted partner and confidant. Regret coursed through him as he realized he had forgotten to inform Briggs about this operation. The weight of his decision pressed upon him, questioning if he had made the right choice to venture into this dangerous mission alone.

Amid his contemplation, Christopher was torn between the desire to reach out to Briggs and the urgency of the present situation. He knew Briggs needed a break from the relentless pursuit of Durango, but the realization that he could have benefitted from Briggs' guidance and support in this critical moment gnawed at him.

As he waited in the shadows, Christopher's mind replayed past conversations and moments shared with Briggs. His thoughts resonated with Their synergy, unspoken understanding, and how they complemented each other in their pursuit of justice. Briggs had always been the voice of reason, offering an alternative perspective, keeping Christopher grounded even in dire circumstances.

Lost in his thoughts, Christopher couldn't help but wonder what Briggs would have done in his shoes. Would he have forged ahead alone, driven by the need to bring Tony to justice and unearth the truth? Or would he have advocated for caution, urging Christopher to wait for backup and not risk everything in one bold move?

The memories of their partnership served as a guiding light, reminding Christopher of the trust they had built over the years. Briggs had entrusted him with crucial decisions in the past, and now it was Christopher's turn to have faith in his capabilities.

Christopher's anticipation grew as the moments stretched into an eternity. He knew that any second now, Bretty would appear, accompanied by Tony. The tension in the air was palpable, every creak and echo in the tunnel heightening his senses.

With each passing moment, Christopher's resolve solidified. He knew he couldn't dwell on missed opportunities or the what-ifs. The mission was already in motion, and he had to trust his instincts and abilities.

As Christopher stood in the dimly lit tunnel, waiting for Bretty to arrive, his senses heightened, alert to any movement or sound. Suddenly, a shadow emerged from the darkness, and his heart skipped a beat. As he focused on the figure, a sinking feeling settled in his stomach. It wasn't Bretty; it was Durango accompanied by his menacing entourage.

Christopher's gaze darted around, his mind racing to comprehend the situation. The tunnel that had once seemed like a place of potential victory now closed in on him, becoming a trap set by his most formidable adversary. It became apparent that he had walked right into their carefully orchestrated ambush.

The tension in the air was palpable, suffocating, as Durango and his men encircled Christopher. The faint glimmers of light reflected off the cold metal of their weapons, the threatening click of safeties being released echoing through the tunnel. Christopher felt the weight of the danger closing in, but he refused to let fear consume him.

Durango, his face twisted into a malevolent smile, took a step forward, his presence commanding authority. The shadowy figures surrounding Christopher emanated an air of silent menace, their eyes fixed unwaveringly on their target.

Christopher's eyes met Durango's, a silent exchange of defiance and determination. He refused to be intimidated and succumbed to the odds stacked against him.

The seconds ticked by agonizingly slow as the standoff continued, the tension stretching like an invisible thread ready to snap. Christopher's mind calculated the risks, analyzing the positions of Durango's men and searching for any vulnerabilities that could be exploited. He needed a plan to seize the initiative and turn the tables in his favour.

Durango's piercing gaze locked onto Christopher, his eyes filled with curiosity and disdain.

"Where is Briggs?" he demanded, his tone laced with chilling intensity. "I don't want you. I want Briggs. Tell me where he is."

Christopher's brow furrowed in confusion. The demand surprised him, his mind racing to understand Durango's motivations. Questions tumbled from Christopher's lips as he sought to comprehend the situation.

"Why Briggs?" Christopher asked, his voice filled with a mix of curiosity and concern. "What does he have to do with all of this?"

Durango's lips curled into a grave, mocking smile. His chuckle reverberated through the tunnel, sending shivers down Christopher's spine. It was a sound that carried years of wicked knowledge, hinting at secrets untold.

"There are many things about Briggs that you don't need to understand, little one," Durango replied cryptically, his voice dripping with enigmatic implications.

Christopher's mind spun, attempting to unravel Durango's words. Yet he was desperate for answers. Christopher pressed. Further, his voice tinged with urgency. "Where is Tony? And what have you done with Bretty?" he demanded.

Durango's expression shifted from amusement to confusion, his brows furrowing. "Tony? Bretty?" he repeated, his voice tinged with bewilderment. "What the fuck are you yapping about, little one?"

Durango's gaze lingered on Christopher. There was a sense of menace in his presence, an unspoken warning that echoed through the stale air of the tunnel.

As Christopher and Durango engaged in their tense standoff, a sudden movement caught their attention. Emerging from the shadows, a tall figure stepped into the tunnel, commanding attention with their presence. It was the same man Christopher had glimpsed at the funeral, who had given the innocent girl the red lotus and the devastating bomb within.

The man's face bore the marks of a tumultuous past, scars etched into his skin like a map of battles fought and wounds endured. His features were chiselled and hardened, exuding a dark, menacing aura that sent a shiver down

Christopher's spine. The intensity in his gaze was unnerving as if he held a reservoir of malevolence within him.

Christopher's breath caught in his throat as he locked eyes with the ominous figure. It was as if time stood still, the weight of their encounter palpable in the air. The rain outside continued to fall, its rhythmic pattern contrasting with the tunnel's tension.

Durango shifted from Christopher to the newcomer, a glimmer of recognition flickering in his eyes. The presence of this formidable individual disrupted the delicate balance of power in the tunnel, injecting an element of uncertainty into an already volatile situation.

With a voice that resonated with an air of authority, the scarred man spoke, his words laced with an unsettling calmness. "Christopher," he began, his tone dripping with menace and familiarity. "I see you've found yourself in quite the predicament."

Christopher's mind raced, attempting to piece together the puzzle of this enigmatic individual. The memories of the funeral resurfaced, the chaos and destruction wrought by the red lotus bomb.

"Who are you?" Christopher demanded, his voice betraying a mixture of apprehension and determination.

The scarred man's lips curled into a chilling smile, revealing a glimpse of the darkness that lay within.

Breaking the silence, the man locked eyes with Christopher and spoke in a firm, commanding tone. "Christopher, where is Briggs?" he asked, his voice revealing a mix of urgency and concern.

Christopher's mind whirled with confusion. Briggs being the focal point of another individual's inquiry only deepened the mystery surrounding his partner's involvement. He quickly collected his thoughts and responded, his voice tinged with uncertainty, "I... I don't know. Briggs has been laid off. We parted ways."

The man's brow furrowed, a flicker of disappointment crossing his features. Christopher could sense the weight of his intent, a sense of urgency driving him to find Briggs.

'The name is Theo. I'm a friend of Briggs.'

"Theo?" Christopher repeated, attempting to reconcile this new piece of information with the web of intrigue surrounding Briggs. "What do you want with him? And what does he have that belongs to you?"

Theo's gaze bore into Christopher. His voice resonated with a touch of dread and menace as he spoke. "Briggs has something of mine. Something that holds great sentimental value," he said curtly. "I've been searching for him, hoping to retrieve it."

"I... I don't know where he is," Christopher stammered. He couldn't help himself from thinking that this was the end of the road for him.

Theo's voice reverberated through the tunnel, filling the confined space with urgency and determination. "Where is Briggs?!" he demanded once more, his tone laced with an underlying intensity that echoed off the damp walls.

Christopher met Theo's gaze head-on, his eyes narrowing with defiance and frustration. The weight of the situation bore heavily on his shoulders, the implications of revealing Briggs's whereabouts fraught with uncertainty. Yet, a fire ignited within Christopher, fueling his resolve to protect his partner and their shared secrets.

With a steely determination, Christopher locked eyes with Theo, his voice laced with conviction. "You, Durango, and all your men can go to hell!" he retorted, his words laced with defiance. "I won't lead you to Briggs."

Theo's features hardened, his scars standing out starkly against his tense expression. The tension in the tunnel reached a crescendo, the air thick with unspoken threats and the clash of conflicting desires.

Theo looked at Durango, and they exchange a knowing glance. He turned back at Christopher, grinned menacingly, and walked out of the tunnel. Durango walked up to Christopher, pulled out his gun and shot him. Three bullets straight to his heart.

As Christopher's body hit the cold, hard floor, a wave of pain surged through him, causing his vision to blur and his senses to falter. Time seemed to slow down, and his life flashed before his eyes in that fleeting moment.

Images and memories cascaded through his mind, each a fragment of his existence. He saw his childhood, filled with laughter and innocence, as he played with friends in the park, his mother's gentle smile watching over him. He remembered the days when he dreamt of becoming a hero, a force for justice in a world plagued by darkness.

But the memories shifted, morphing into moments of determination and resilience as he trained to become an agent, honing his skills and dedicating himself to protecting others. He recalled the countless missions, the high-stakes situations where he had risked his life to uphold the law and bring criminals to justice. Each memory carried a weight, a testament to his unwavering commitment.

Through the haze of pain, Christopher's gaze remained fixed on the figures surrounding him. Durango's men, the faceless adversaries who had cornered him in this desolate tunnel. One by one, they turned their backs and faded into the shadows, their purpose fulfilled. Christopher felt a profound loneliness wash over him as he realized the gravity of his situation. He was alone, his strength ebbing away, surrounded by darkness.

As his vision blended with the dimly lit tunnel, the world around him distorted, like a surreal painting. The flickering shadows danced and merged with his fading consciousness, creating a haunting backdrop to his final moments. The distant echoes of Durango's laughter reverberated through the air, mocking and cruel.

And then, a final word pierced the veil of Christopher's fading awareness. Durango's voice, dripping with satisfaction, delivered those haunting words. "Bretty! Good job!" The realization hit Christopher like a heavy blow. Bretty, the woman he had trusted, the woman he had shared moments of intimacy and vulnerability with, had betrayed him. The weight of her deception settled upon his wounded heart, leaving him with a bitter taste of betrayal.

As darkness enveloped him, Christopher's body went limp, surrendering to the oblivion that awaited him. His breathing grew shallow, and the rhythm of his heartbeat slowed. In his final moments, he clung to the fragments of his resolve, finding solace in the knowledge that he had fought for what he believed in, even in the face of betrayal.

Christopher's mind drifted to Briggs, his former partner and confidant, who had stood by his side through countless trials. Regret washed over him for not contacting Briggs or sharing his suspicions and concerns.

In the fading embers of consciousness, Christopher's thoughts turned to the unfinished battle against Durango, the mysterious puppet master pulling the strings from the shadows. He prayed that his sacrifice would not be in vain, that his death would fuel the fire of justice and lead to Durango's downfall.

Christopher embraced the darkness, knowing that his journey had ended. His body lay still, a fallen hero in a world marred by corruption and treachery.

CHAPTER EIGHT

Briggs jolted awake, his heart pounding in his chest. He took a moment to gather his bearings, reassuring himself that it was just a nightmare. Sweat glistened on his forehead, evidence of the fear that had gripped him in his sleep. He glanced around the room, his eyes scanning the familiar surroundings, seeking solace in the reality surrounding him.

Beside him, Rachel, sensed his distress and woke from her slumber. Concern etched on her face, she reached out and placed a comforting hand on his back, her touch offering reassurance during his turmoil. Her soothing voice coaxed him, coaxing him back to a state of calm and sleep.

Briggs settled back onto the bed, his mind still racing with the vivid images from his nightmare. The figure of Theo, with his menacing presence and scarred face, haunted his thoughts. The memory of seeing Christopher apprehended and shot played on a loop, causing a shiver to run down his spine.

Despite Rachel's comforting presence, sleep eluded him. The echoes of his dream reverberated through his mind, leaving an unsettling residue. He couldn't shake the feeling of unease, the lingering sense that danger lurked just beyond the edges of his consciousness.

Lost in his thoughts, Briggs stared at the ceiling, the moon's faint glow casting a soft light across the room.

With the first light of dawn on the horizon, Briggs took a deep breath, his eyes fixed on the path ahead. He would find the answers and ensure Christopher was okay.

As the morning sun peeked through the windows of Rachel's apartment, its gentle rays danced across the room, casting a warm glow on the furniture and infusing the space with a sense of tranquillity. The aroma of freshly brewed coffee filled the air, intermingling with the sweet scent of waffles sizzling on the griddle.

In the kitchen, Rachel moved gracefully and purpose, donning an apron that had seen countless breakfasts prepared with love. Her nimble hands expertly flipped the golden-brown waffles, their edges crisping to perfection. The rhythmic clinking of utensils against bowls and the soft hum of the refrigerator created a soothing symphony, complementing the peaceful morning ambience.

Briggs sat at the dining table and watched Rachel with admiration. Her tousled hair cascaded over her shoulders, framing her face like a golden halo. The morning light accentuated her features, casting a soft glow on her gentle smile. The love and care she poured into every action filled the room, warming Briggs's heart.

As Rachel set the plate of waffles on the table, the aroma enveloped the room, enticing Briggs's senses. He took a moment to appreciate the spread before him: the golden waffles adorned with a drizzle of maple syrup, a sprinkle of powdered sugar, and a vibrant assortment of berries cascading down the side.

Their eyes met, and a silent understanding passed between them. It was a moment of shared appreciation, a recognition of life's simple joys, even in the face of uncertainty. Briggs's heart swelled with gratitude for Rachel's presence in his life, for her unwavering support and love.

With a contented sigh, Briggs picked up his fork and savoured the first bite of the crisp waffle. The flavours exploded on his tongue, a delightful combination of sweetness and warmth. As he chewed, his gaze never wavered from Rachel, who moved about the kitchen with effortless grace, a portrait of domestic bliss.

They engaged in light conversation between bites, their words floating through the air like a gentle melody. Briggs listened intently, captivated by Rachel's voice, her words weaving a tapestry of comfort and reassurance. Their connection transcended the confines of the breakfast table, a bond forged through shared experiences and unspoken support.

The morning sun continued to bathe the room in its golden light, casting playful shadows that danced on the walls. It was as if the universe conspired to create a moment of respite, a sanctuary from the outside world, where the weight of their responsibilities temporarily faded away.

As Briggs took the last bite of his waffle, savouring the flavours on his palate, Rachel rose from her seat and untied her apron, revealing her nurse attire. The sight caught Briggs off guard, his eyebrows knitting together in curiosity and concern.

His gaze shifted from the discarded apron to Rachel, who stood tall and determined, her eyes reflecting a sense of urgency. She approached Briggs, her steps purposeful yet gentle, and touched his shoulder.

"There's been an emergency at the hospital," she explained, her voice steady but tinged with a hint of worry. "They found a man in critical condition in the tunnels."

Briggs nodded as he absorbed her words, his mind racing to comprehend the situation unfolding before him.

"I have to go, Briggs," she said, her voice laced with determination.

Reluctantly, Briggs nodded, understanding the gravity of the situation. Rachel leaned in, pressing a tender kiss on his cheek, leaving a trace of warmth and affection.

As she turned to leave, Briggs watched her with a mix of pride and concern. His admiration for her dedication and strength swelled within him, yet he couldn't shake the worry that enveloped his heart.

The room felt emptier without her presence, the lingering scent of breakfast fading into the air. Briggs sighed, his mind wandering to the previous night's events, the haunting image of Theo and the weight of unfinished business weighing heavily on his thoughts.

After finishing his meal, Briggs stood up from the dining table, feeling a sense of restlessness tugging at his being. He needed a moment of solitude to clear his mind and gather his thoughts. The vibrant sunlight streaming through the windows beckoned him, promising a brief respite from the worries that weighed on his shoulders.

Briggs approached the backdoor, stepping out onto the small but cosy backyard. The sun's warmth greeted him like an old friend, its golden rays enveloping his body, providing a comforting embrace.

He took a deep breath and marvelled at the day's beauty. The London sky stretched above him, adorned with scattered fluffy clouds that added a touch of whimsy to the scene. The air felt crisp and invigorating, carrying the fragrance of blooming flowers and the distant scent of freshly cut grass.

The backyard was a peaceful sanctuary, a small oasis amidst the bustling city. Vibrant green plants adorned the borders, their leaves swaying gently in the breeze. A modest wooden bench stood under a blossoming tree, offering a place of solace and reflection.

Briggs walked over to the bench and sat, his eyes closed, and his face turned towards the sun. The sunlight seemed to infuse him with renewed energy, revitalizing his spirit.

Birds chirped melodiously in the distance, their songs a harmonious backdrop to his thoughts. He let his mind wander, allowing the moment's tranquillity to envelop him. In these moments of stillness, he found clarity and the strength to face the challenges ahead.

The bustling city noises seemed distant from this tranquil retreat. The occasional car passing by on the nearby street became a mere murmur in the background. It was as if time stood still, offering Briggs a temporary respite from the world's demands.

With each breath he took, Briggs felt a sense of peace. The worries and uncertainties that plagued his mind dissipated, replaced by a calm determination. The weight on his shoulders lightened, and his thoughts became clearer.

As Briggs basked in the soothing embrace of the sun, his phone buzzed, interrupting the moment's tranquillity. With a curious glance, he retrieved his phone and saw Matthias's name flashing on the screen. A smile formed on his lips as he answered the call, eager to catch up with his former partner. He had Matthias had shared a case of weapon smuggling and had formed countless memories with during their investigation.

"Matthias!" Briggs greeted, his voice filled with excitement.

Matthias's voice boomed from the other end of the line, full of exuberance and contagious energy. "Briggs, my old buddy! How's life treating you, mate?"

The banter between the two friends flowed effortlessly, their voices intertwining with a camaraderie that only years of shared experiences could forge. Their conversation was a mixture of catching up, reminiscing about past cases, and sharing lighthearted anecdotes that brought forth hearty laughter.

Briggs leaned back on the bench, his gaze fixed on the dancing leaves above him, as he listened to Matthias's hilarious tales and witty remarks. Each word from his old partner sparked joy, washing away the remnants of worry and uncertainty that had clung to his mind earlier.

They spoke of their respective lives since parting ways, sharing snippets of their journeys. Matthias recounted his recent misadventures, regaling Briggs with tales of mishaps and humorous encounters that left them both in stitches.

The conversation flowed effortlessly, as if no time had passed between them. They reminisced about their escapades during the weapon smuggling investigation, recalling the near-misses, daring chases, and the countless cups of coffee shared in stakeout cars.

Briggs's laughter echoed through the backyard as Matthias's words filled the airwaves. It was a moment of respite, a reminder of the bonds forged in the crucible of their shared profession.

'Hey, Matthias, speaking of old times, guess who resurfaced on my radar recently?'

'Do tell. You know I'm all ears for any exciting updates from the world of crime-fighting.'

'It's Tony, the notorious weapon smuggler we spent months tracking down. I have a feeling he's on the run again. We might have to dust off our investigation skills.'

'Tony? Are you sure about that, Briggs? I hate to break it to you, but Tony is no longer a threat. He's dead.'

'Dead? Are you serious, Matthias? When did that happen?'

'That was about two months ago, Briggs. We received Intel that he got shot by one of his ex-girlfriends. Seems she was also sent to him.'

'Hold on, Matthias. I'm having trouble processing this. Are you saying that Tony was assassinated by one of his ex-girlfriends? And that she was working for someone within his criminal ranks?

'I wish I had better news, Briggs, but that's exactly what happened. Tony's ex-girlfriend, who had connections to his criminal association, was sent to eliminate him. It seems that someone higher up in the chain of command felt threatened by Tony's potential to expose certain activities.'

'This is unbelievable. Who could be behind such an act?'

'That's the million-dollar question, my friend. We're still trying to piece together all the details. The investigation is ongoing, but it's a delicate situation.'

'This is mind-boggling. Tony's own people turned against him. It's like something out of a movie. Did they know that we were closing in on him?'

'It's hard to say, Briggs. The timing does seem suspicious, doesn't it? It's possible they got wind of our investigation and took drastic measures to protect themselves. Tony must have been a liability in their eyes.'

'Thanks, Matthias. For this information.'

'You can count on me, Briggs.'

After ending the phone call with Matthias, Briggs couldn't shake off the unsettling feeling that engulfed him. The revelation about Tony's assassination by his ex-girlfriend left him questioning everything he thought he knew. His mind wandered back to his conversation with Lainy, Tony's neighbour, during their investigation.

Elainhad mentioned seeing Bretty at Tony's apartment, using a silencer. At the time, Briggs had brushed it off as a minor detail, focusing on bringing Tony to justice. But now, the pieces started to fall into place. Bretty must have been playing a dangerous game, working as a double agent.

The realization hit Briggs like a ton of bricks. He had trusted Bretty. How could he have been so blind?

Briggs paced back and forth in Racheal's apartment, his mind racing with conflicting emotions. He couldn't believe he had been deceived so profoundly. He questioned his judgment, wondering how he could have mixed up the signs. Briggs couldn't help but feel a sense of betrayal from Bretty and himself for falling into her web of deception.

As he paced, he tried to piece together the puzzle. Bretty's sudden disappearance after their mission at Durango's place, her haste when they apprehended her at Tony's place, and the fear in her eyes made sense now. She knew her true identity as Tony's killer would be exposed, and she needed to disappear before anyone discovered the truth.

Briggs wondered how deep Bretty's involvement with Durango went. Was she a mere pawn in their game, or did she have a more significant role? The thought of her potentially leading them into a trap and risking their lives made his blood boil.

He sat down on the couch, staring blankly at the wall. The weight of the situation pressed heavily on his shoulders. He knew he couldn't let his personal emotions cloud his judgment. Bretty had to be stopped, and he had to find the truth behind her betrayal.

As Briggs was lost in his thoughts, his phone rang, jolting him back to reality. It was Racheal. He quickly answered the call and asked what the matter was.

'Briggs, it's Racheal. There's something... something happened. It's Christopher.' he sensed a hint of agitation in her voice

'What's happened? Is he okay?

'No, he's not okay. He's in the hospital. He was shot... three times in the heart. They're doing an emergency heart surgery for him right now.

Racheal's words hit Briggs like a punch to the gut. Christopher was hospitalised, having been shot three times in the heart. The gravity of the situation weighed heavily upon him, and he could feel his legs growing weak. He leaned against the nearest surface, feeling a sense of despair wash over him. Christopher, his partner and friend, lay fighting for his life.

'What? How... how did this happen?'

'I'm unsure of all the details, but he was ambushed. It's serious, Briggs.'

Briggs hung up the phone, his mind reeling with mixed emotions. He couldn't fathom the idea of Christopher fighting for his life, lying in a hospital bed. It felt like a nightmare, a cruel twist of fate.

His legs felt heavy as he contemplated the situation. Sinking back into a nearby chair, he tried to gather his thoughts. Briggs realized that he couldn't waste any more time. Pushing through the despair threatening to consume him, he rose from the chair and went to the door.

Briggs arrived at the hospital, his heart pounding with anticipation and trepidation. As he stepped through the entrance, the sterile scent of disinfectant and the echoes of bustling activity overwhelmed his senses. The familiar smell of antiseptic mixed with the unmistakable atmosphere of a place where life and death intertwined.

He couldn't shake off the gloomy feeling that hung in the air, as if the weight of all the pain and suffering of the patients permeated the walls. It made him feel slightly nauseous, but he pushed through, driven by his determination to see Christopher.

Racheal met him in the lobby. Her eyes held a mix of worry and exhaustion, yet she managed a reassuring smile. She led Briggs through the maze of corridors, their footsteps echoing against the linoleum floor.

The further they walked, the heavier the silence grew, interrupted only by the occasional sound of medical equipment and hushed conversations. It was a stark contrast to the chaos of the outside world, as if time had stood still within these sterile walls.

Finally, they arrived at the ward where Christopher lay. Briggs peered through the small window on the door, his gaze fixed on his friend's motionless figure. Christopher appeared fragile, and vulnerable, yet there was a resilience in how he lay there, as if fighting against the darkness that threatened to consume him.

His eyes traced the lines and tubes connected to Christopher's body, the steady beep of the heart monitor as a reminder of the fragility of life. It was a bittersweet sight, knowing that the very instrument keeping Christopher alive also highlighted the precariousness of his situation.

Briggs felt a lump form in his throat, his emotions welling up as he struggled to comprehend the gravity of the situation. Memories of their adventures, shared laughter, and unspoken understanding flooded his mind. Christopher had always been there for him, and now it was his turn to be there for his friend.

Racheal gently placed her hand on Briggs' shoulder, breaking his trance. Her touch provided a small solace, reminding him he wasn't alone. They were all united in their support for Christopher.

Christopher lay motionless on the hospital bed, his body engulfed by a labyrinth of tubes and wires. The sterile hospital room hummed with the soft whirring of machines, each monitoring his vital signs and fighting to keep him connected to the realm of the living.

His face, once vibrant and full of life, was now concealed partially by a hair net that held his dark locks in place. The pallor of his skin stood in stark contrast against the crisp white sheets, a haunting reminder of the battle he was currently waging.

His chest rose and fell rhythmically, aided by the mechanical assistance of a ventilator. Each breath seemed fragile, as if inhaling and exhaling was a delicate dance between life and death. The sight of him in this state evoked a profound sense of vulnerability, a reminder of the fragility of human existence.

The tubes that snaked across his body were lifelines, connecting him to various monitors and life-support systems. Intravenous lines delivered vital fluids and medications, nourishing his weakened form. The beeping of the machines kept a steady cadence, a symphony of hope amidst the uncertainty that filled the room.

Around his wrist, a pulse oximeter clung tightly, continuously monitoring his oxygen saturation levels. Its glowing display provided a small measure of reassurance, a visual confirmation that his body still fought to hold on, that life still coursed through his veins.

His face bore the marks of the ordeal he had endured. Shadows beneath his closed eyes betrayed the exhaustion and pain hidden within. Bruises and abrasions marked his skin, remnants of the violent encounter that had brought him to this precipice between life and death.

Despite his fragile state, a sense of resilience emanated from him. His features, though pale and marred, still retained a hint of the strength and determination that defined his character. It was as if his spirit fought alongside his physical body, refusing to yield to the darkness that threatened to consume him.

In such vulnerability, the room seemed to hold its breath, as if time was suspended. Nurses moved gently, tending to Christopher's needs, adjusting the equipment, and offering silent prayers for his recovery.

The soft glow of the overhead lights illuminated the room, casting a gentle halo around Christopher's form. It starkly contrasted the turmoil within, the battle between life and death, hope and despair. The serenity of the lighting seemed incongruous, as if the world outside the room remained oblivious to the fierce struggle within its walls.

The weight of the situation hung heavily in the air, a palpable heaviness that pressed upon the hearts of all who entered the room. Time seemed to stretch, each second pregnant with hope and anxiety, as they waited for signs of improvement, indicating that Christopher's body was responding to the treatments.

As the hours passed, there were small glimmers of progress. Vital signs stabilised, oxygen saturation levels climbed, and the whispers of hope grew louder.

CHAPTER NINE

He could still feel the weight of his uniform, the crispness of the fabric against his skin, and the smell of the military barracks that hung in the air. As a new young unit member, he had faced his fair share of physical and emotional challenges.

One aspect that had been particularly difficult for Briggs was his stature. Standing at a shorter height and possessing a lanky build, he had become the target of jesters and mockeries from his fellow soldiers. Their taunts cut deep, chipping away his self-confidence and fueling his doubts.

But amidst the sea of teasing and laughter, one figure had stood out, a tall young man who possessed a commanding presence. This tall comrade had noticed the unfair treatment directed towards Briggs and swiftly intervened. His stern voice and unwavering determination had silenced the jesters, extinguishing their hurtful remarks. His name was Theo.

Theo, recognizing the potential in Briggs, had taken him under his wing. He became a guide and a friend, offering guidance and support during those formative years. With his broad shoulders and towering stature, Theo had become a protective shield against all ridicule that threatened to consume Briggs.

Together, they had trained relentlessly, honing their skills and pushing each other to new heights. Theo's strength and confidence became a source of inspiration for Briggs, propelling him forward and igniting a fire within him. Under Theo's guidance, he grew physically and mentally, shedding the insecurities that once plagued him.

Their bond extended beyond the battlefield, as they shared moments of camaraderie and laughter amidst the harsh realities of war. In the face of danger, they stood side by side, their trust unshakable, their dedication unwavering. Theo's presence gave Briggs a sense of belonging, that he was not alone in an unforgiving world.

Briggs recalled how Theo's friendship had helped him personally and earned their fellow soldiers' respect. His fierce determination and unwavering loyalty had elevated him to a position of admiration within the unit. Many looked up to him, seeking guidance and reassurance in times of uncertainty.

Their shared experiences forged a unique understanding and developed a playful camaraderie that grew stronger with time. One aspect that became a running joke between the two was their height difference. While Briggs had grown taller and more experienced, he still fell short of Theo's impressive stature.

In good spirits, Theo affectionately dubbed Briggs "Beetle Briggs," a playful nod to the incident when a beetle had unexpectedly flown onto Briggs, causing him to flinch and inadvertently dodge an enemy bullet. It was a moment that had saved his life, and they laughed about it often, appreciating the unpredictable nature of warfare and the strange occurrences that can alter the course of events.

Briggs, in turn, nicknamed Theo "Tree Theo," a lighthearted reference to his habit of finding refuge and cover behind trees during intense battles. It symbolised their shared understanding and ability to adapt and utilize their surroundings to their advantage.

Their height difference was not merely a source of jest; it was a source of the diversity of their skills and their complementary roles on the battlefield. Briggs admired Theo's ability to utilise the environment to his advantage, often using trees as protection and a vantage point. His tall stature gave him a strategic advantage, allowing him to survey the battlefield and guide Briggs through the chaos.

On the other hand, Briggs's smaller stature allowed him to manoeuvre swiftly and navigate tight spaces that Theo couldn't reach. His agility and quick reflexes proved invaluable in close-quarter combat, enabling him to evade enemy fire and strike with precision. They recognized and appreciated the unique qualities they brought to their partnership, understanding that their differences only enhanced their effectiveness as a team.

As the war raged, their trust and reliance on one another grew stronger. They became more than battle companions; they became brothers in arms, ready to sacrifice anything for the other's well-being. The other would leap to their defence without hesitation when one faced danger. Their unity and unwavering loyalty formed an unbreakable shield against the perils surrounding them.

During the chaos and brutality of war, Briggs and Theo found solace in their shared journey. They had witnessed each other's triumphs and scars, experiencing firsthand the fragility of life and the magnitude of sacrifice. This shared understanding deepened their connection, forging a bond that transcended the bounds of ordinary friendship.

As the years passed, circumstances led Briggs to make the difficult decision to leave the army, bidding farewell to Theo and their shared life on the battlefield. While Theo couldn't help but feel a pang of sadness at their parting, he knew deep down that their paths would cross again one day.

Having honed his skills and gained invaluable experience in the military, Briggs found himself handpicked by the government to join a secret and elite government force. This force, led by the renowned Andrew Edge, operated in the shadows, tackling covert missions that required the utmost discretion and skill. At that time, Alexander Q, now known as a powerful figure and the head of the organisation, was still an agent, albeit a senior one.

Briggs entered this new phase of his life with determination and an unwavering commitment to serve his country. He navigated his way through the ranks of the secret force, impressing his superiors with his exceptional abilities and dedication. With each successful mission, he cemented his reputation as a rising star, becoming known for his tenacity, resourcefulness, and an uncanny ability to solve even the most complex cases.

Briggs's track record was remarkable. He possessed a unique talent for unravelling mysteries and bringing criminals to justice, leaving no loose ends in his wake. It was a feat that garnered attention and admiration, especially considering that Alexander Q himself had been the only agent with a similar record throughout his years of service.

Andrew Edge, the esteemed leader of the secret government force, had been closely observing Briggs' remarkable performance and exceptional abilities. Impressed by Briggs' unwavering dedication, resourcefulness, and unparalleled track record, Andrew saw the potential for great things in him.

Recognizing Briggs' talent and the need for swift action, Andrew decided to elevate him through the ranks, bypassing the usual waiting period that senior officers deemed necessary. This unexpected promotion caused a stir among the higher-ranking officers who believed that Briggs should have followed the conventional path of gradual progression.

Voices of dissent emerged, expressing concerns over the unconventional decision to fast-track Briggs' ascent. Some argued that he had yet to accumulate enough experience, while others questioned the fairness of this leapfrogging advancement. However, Andrew remained steadfast in his belief in Briggs' capabilities and dismissed their complaints.

Andrew understood that exceptional circumstances called for exceptional measures. He recognized that Briggs possessed unique skills that set him apart. His impeccable record and the results he achieved spoke for themselves. Andrew saw a rare combination of intellect, adaptability, and a relentless pursuit of excellence in Briggs.

As Briggs assumed his new role, his responsibilities were paramount. He was entrusted with the task of overseeing top-secret government facilities, safeguarding sensitive information that held the potential to impact national security. His ability to handle such crucial responsibilities with unwavering commitment made him an invaluable asset to the organisation.

In addition to his duties within the facilities, Briggs was also assigned intricate coded international missions on behalf of various government agencies in the Western world. These missions demanded utmost secrecy and a high level of expertise and finesse to navigate the complex landscape of international espionage. Armed with his exceptional analytical skills and sharp intuition, Briggs tackled each mission with precision and resolve.

For Briggs, this was the culmination of a lifelong dream. He found himself in a position that mirrored his childhood fantasies—the opportunity to operate within high-tech facilities, engage in intricate coded operations across the globe, and become the real-life embodiment of the legendary James Bond. It was an exhilarating realisation for him, a chance to embrace the allure of being the coolest agent in the field.

With his new responsibilities, Briggs found himself traversing the world, immersing himself in exotic locales, and encountering various cultures. These missions tested his skills and resourcefulness and allowed him to experience the thrill of exploration and adventure. He became a true globetrotter, navigating through the shadows of clandestine operations with style and finesse.

As he ventured from one mission to another, Briggs's charisma and charm often attracted the attention of beautiful women. His profession's enigmatic allure and undeniable magnetism made him an intriguing figure in their eyes. His encounters with these captivating women became a source of envy for his fellow senior detectives, who couldn't help but express their dismay at Briggs seemingly living the life of a modern-day playboy.

Despite the murmurs of discontent, Andrew Edge, the leader who had recognized Briggs' potential, remained steadfast in his support. He saw beyond the surface-level judgments, understanding that Briggs's competence and commitment to his mission were unwavering. Andrew valued results above all else, and Briggs consistently delivered.

Though tempting, Briggs's encounters with beautiful women never distracted him from his duty. He understood the importance of maintaining focus and professionalism, recognizing that his role demanded unwavering dedication. The allure of his profession and the attention it garnered served as a backdrop to the more significant purpose he served—the safeguarding of his nation's security and the pursuit of justice.

While his adventures and encounters may have invoked envy among his peers, Briggs never lost sight of his purpose. He understood that his role was not about personal gratification or indulgence but serving a greater cause. The experiences he gained and the knowledge he acquired throughout his journeys shaped him into a more seasoned and effective agent.

Briggs understood that being the coolest agent meant more than just the thrilling escapades and a suave demeanour. It meant being meticulous in planning, maintaining exceptional physical fitness, and continuously honing his skills. He spent countless hours refining his marksmanship, hand-to-hand combat techniques, and mastering the art of stealth. These efforts were not driven by vanity but by a genuine desire to be the best in his field.

As he continued to excel, Briggs inspired younger agents, his name whispered in hushed admiration throughout the agency. His journey from a young soldier ridiculed for his lanky stature to an esteemed covert operative was a testament to hard work, determination, and the ability to seize opportunities.

The technological advancements at his disposal played a significant role in his achievements. The state-of-the-art gadgets and surveillance equipment gave him a decisive edge in the field. With each operation, he harnessed the power of these tools, leveraging them to gain critical information, outmanoeuvre adversaries, and protect national interests.

Through it all, Briggs never lost sight of the core values instilled in him from his early military training days. Integrity, loyalty, and the pursuit of justice were the driving forces behind his actions. He knew that his role transcended personal desires and was ultimately about safeguarding the greater good.

While his life may have appeared glamorous, it was rife with sacrifices and emotional tolls. The constant pressure, the ever-present danger, and the weight of responsibility wore on him. There were sleepless nights, moments of doubt, and the haunting memories of fallen comrades. But Briggs persevered, knowing that the cause he fought for was for the greater good.

At the peak of his success, Theo arrived at the organisation. This marked a significant moment for both him and Briggs. While they had once been inseparable as friends and comrades on the battlefield, the dynamics had shifted as Briggs now held a superior position within the secret force. Despite their history, Theo understood and respected the chain of command that governed their roles.

Although physically separated, the bond between Theo and Briggs remained strong. They recognized the value of their friendship and shared battlefield experiences. Despite the geographical distance, they made a concerted effort to stay in touch, keeping the lines of communication open through letters, encrypted messages, and occasional rendezvous when their schedules aligned.

Theo, while having great respect for Briggs as his superior, didn't forget the trust and support that Briggs had shown him during their time as soldiers. Briggs, in turn, recognized Theo's capabilities and the unique perspective he brought to the table. The bond forged in their past experiences continued to be a source of inspiration and motivation for both of them.

As time passed and the intelligence community expanded, tensions rose within its ranks. The diverse pool of agents from various countries all over the world added a layer of complexity to the already intricate dynamics.

One of the primary factors contributing to the escalating tension was the clash of national interests. Agents were inherently driven by the objectives and priorities of their home countries, which often clashed with the goals of other nations. This inherent conflict of interest created a fertile ground for animosity and mistrust among agents from different countries.

Additionally, the issue of bias in ranking and promotion further exacerbated the divide within the intelligence community. Some officers believed that the ranking system favoured agents from Western democratic nations over their counterparts from other nations. This perception led to a sense of resentment and disillusionment among agents who felt their contributions were undervalued or overlooked due to their nationality or geopolitical affiliations.

These internal divisions and biases were fueled, to some extent, by the financial backing and support that the agency received from Western democratic governments. This financial dependence created a power dynamic that inadvertently favoured agents from countries aligned with these governments, further deepening the inequity and marginalisation of agents from other nations.

As tensions escalated, cliques began to form within the agency. Agents aligned themselves with like-minded colleagues who shared similar nationalities or political ideologies. These cliques, often operating within informal networks, further perpetuated the divisions within the intelligence community.

The emergence of these divisions and rivalries posed a significant challenge to the agency's effectiveness. The growing animosity and mistrust among agents compromised the spirit of cooperation and collaboration, vital in counteracting global threats. The once-unified community began to fracture, with agents prioritising their interests and national agendas over collective security.

In the wake of escalating tensions and divisions within the intelligence community, Briggs and Theo found themselves on opposite sides of a growing ideological rift. Their once-strong bond began to fracture as their differing perspectives clashed.

Having risen through the ranks and benefited from the system, Briggs aligned himself with the agency's decisions and policies. He believed that the hierarchy and promotion structure was fair and based on meritocracy. In his view, he had worked diligently to earn the position he was given and deserved the recognition and opportunities that came with it.

On the other hand, Theo grew increasingly disillusioned with what he perceived as a biased and unfair system. He felt that many deserving agents were overlooked or marginalised due to their nationality or political affiliations. His experiences and observations made him question the ranking process's integrity and transparency.

As tensions mounted, their diverging opinions on the state of the intelligence community reached a breaking point. Theo accused Briggs of being blinded by his own biases and failing to see the struggles and injustices faced by agents beneath him. He argued that Briggs's position of privilege had shielded him from the harsh realities experienced by many others within the agency.

Feeling attacked and misunderstood, Briggs defended his accomplishments and the integrity of his position. He vehemently rejected Theo's accusations, asserting his success resulted from hard work and dedication. He argued that Theo's discontent stemmed from personal frustrations and a failure to recognize the complexities of the intelligence community.

The heated argument emotionally affected their friendship, as both men felt their loyalty and trust betrayed. The once inseparable duo found themselves at odds, their shared experiences and camaraderie overshadowed by their conflicting perspectives. Resentment and bitterness clouded their interactions, and they grew distant.

Theo, disillusioned by the system he perceived as flawed, sought alternative paths to make a difference. He became involved in independent investigative work, seeking to expose corruption and promote transparency within the intelligence community. Although his efforts were met with resistance and obstacles, he remained resolute in bringing about meaningful change.

The intelligence community soon came to their moment of reckoning—a realisation that the system needed reform. The concerns raised by officers regarding biases and favouritism were taken seriously, prompting a reshuffling of roles and a sincere effort to address the issues at hand.

Under the leadership of the agency's senior officials, a comprehensive review was conducted to identify and rectify the flaws within the ranking and promotion system. Measures were put in place to ensure a fair and unbiased evaluation process, with greater emphasis on merit and performance rather than political affiliations or nationality.

As part of this reform, Theo, who had long felt undervalued and overlooked, was finally recognized for his skills and potential. He was elevated to a higher position. Other deserving agents who had been overshadowed also received the recognition and opportunities they had long deserved.

Theo's newfound position brought him face-to-face with Briggs once again. Despite the bitter history and their previous falling-out, they found themselves on the same mission to Cameroon—a critical operation to retrieve hidden files that the shadow Russian agency had concealed.

Arriving in Cameroon, Briggs and Theo faced the challenges of navigating a complex and dangerous environment. The mission required them to utilize their unique skills, instincts, and knowledge gained from years of experience. As they delved deeper into the mission, the weight of their past disagreements faded, replaced by a shared sense of purpose and a common goal.

Briggs and Theo were faced with a complex and dangerous environment. The country's dense jungles and intricate network of underground operations presented significant challenges. However, their shared history and previous experiences of working together provided a foundation of trust and understanding, enabling them to collaborate effectively.

As they ventured deeper into the heart of Cameroon, the mission posed unexpected challenges and risks. They encountered treacherous terrain, encountered local resistance, and had to navigate through a web of deception and danger.

As Briggs and Theo reached the location where their clues and findings revealed the hidden files, anticipation and adrenaline coursed through their veins. The facility before them was dimly lit, with a sense of secrecy and danger hanging in the air. They knew that their mission's success relied on their ability to retrieve the files swiftly and efficiently.

Briggs stepped forward, his eyes locked on the file sitting on a stand in the centre of the room. It was a crucial piece of information with secret codes that would unlock the facilities of the Russian shadowy organisation. The intelligence community needed this to turn their weapon against them.

Briggs's hand instinctively reached for his wrist, where a sleek, intelligent wristwatch adorned his arm. This device had been his trusted companion throughout countless missions, concealing various advanced capabilities.

Realizing the importance of verifying and saving the file's contents, Briggs swiftly activated his wristwatch's scanning function. With a flick of his finger, a holographic interface materialized above the watch's face, illuminating the room with a soft blue glow.

Briggs's eyes darted between the holographic display and the physical file he held. As the scanning process initiated, intricate lines of code and data streamed across the hologram, analyzing the file's contents with unparalleled speed and precision.

Finally, the holographic display blinked, indicating that the scan was complete. Briggs's heart raced with anticipation as he read the results that materialized before his eyes. A mix of relief and apprehension washed over him as he processed the information revealed by his wristwatch.

The scan confirmed the file's authenticity and saved it in Brigg's wristwatch.

As Briggs reached out to tuck the file in, he felt a sudden impact against his chest. The force of the blow sent him sprawling to the floor, his vision momentarily blurred with surprise and confusion.

It was Theo, who had knocked him down. Briggs stared up at Theo, a mixture of disbelief and disappointment across his face. He couldn't comprehend the sudden betrayal from someone he had trusted and fought alongside.

Surprised and disoriented, Briggs looked up to see Theo standing over him. Confusion clouded Briggs's face as he tried to comprehend the sudden turn of events. His mind raced with questions, wondering why Theo had resorted to such an aggressive act.

"Why, Theo?" Briggs managed to utter, his voice laced with a tinge of hurt and confusion. He struggled to find an explanation for Theo's actions, desperately hoping that there was a justifiable reason behind the betrayal.

Theo, however, remained silent, his expression guarded and unreadable. He snatched the file from Briggs's hands and clutched the file tightly in his hands. The room grew heavy with tension as the two former allies faced off, their eyes locked in a battle of conflicting emotions.

Struggling to regain his composure, Briggs locked eyes with Theo, a mixture of betrayal and bewilderment evident in his gaze. He found himself searching for answers in the depths of

Theo's expression, hoping to uncover the motive behind his friend's unexpected betrayal.

Theo's expression remained stoic, his grip on the file tightening. After a moment of silence that seemed to stretch on forever, he finally spoke, his voice laced with bitterness and determination. "Briggs, I had to do this. There's something bigger at stake here, something you can't comprehend. I've seen things, learned things, and I can't allow this information to fall into the wrong hands."

The weight of Theo's words hung heavily in the air, leaving Briggs struggling to process the depth of their meaning. Questions swirled in his mind, and unease settled deep within him. He had always known Theo to be an honourable and dedicated agent, but this sudden shift in allegiance left him questioning everything they had shared.

Struggling to process this unexpected revelation, Briggs found his voice amidst the turmoil. "Theo, what do you mean? How can you work for them? We were on the same side!"

Theo's expression remained stoic. With a heavy sigh, he began. "Briggs, I was in a precarious situation during our time apart. Disillusioned by the division within our ranks, the organisation I worked for sought alliances elsewhere. We teamed up with certain Russian agents who shared our goal of combating global threats."

Briggs listened intently, his mind reeling with the implications of Theo's confession. He had always known Theo to be fiercely loyal and committed to their cause, and the revelation of his newfound allegiance struck at the core of their friendship.

Theo continued, his voice filled with a mix of regret and determination. "I became a double agent, tasked with infiltrating their ranks and gaining their trust. It was a difficult decision, but I believed that by working from within, I could gather invaluable intelligence and potentially uncover the truth behind this conspiracy that threatens us all."

A wave of conflicting emotions washed over Briggs. Anger, betrayal, and a tinge of understanding warred within him as he tried to reconcile his memories of the friend he once knew with the person standing before him.

"Theo," Briggs finally managed to speak, his voice laced with disappointment and confusion, "What have you done?"

"Briggs, I wish I could have trusted you completely. But in this dangerous game, trust becomes a fragile commodity. I had to keep my cover intact, even if it meant keeping secrets from those closest to me."

Theo lifted up the file in his hands happily. 'This belongs to me. It will get me really far in life.' he said with a smug smile and made to walk out.

Theo's words lingered in the air. Briggs's expression hardened in an unexpected turn of events, and a determined glint appeared in his eyes. Without warning, he launched himself at Theo, his training and instincts taking over. The element of surprise worked in his favour, and Theo was caught off guard as Briggs knocked him to the ground.

The struggle for the file became a physical and mental battle between two former friends turned rivals. Theo, fueled by a mixture of anger and betrayal, fought back with equal intensity. Each blow and countermove carried the weight of their shattered camaraderie. Briggs recovered the file from Theo and ran out.

The chase unfolded through the labyrinthine corridors of the facility, the tension mounting with every passing moment. Briggs's heart pounded in his chest as he sprinted ahead, the file clutched tightly in his hand. His determination unyielding, Theo pursued him relentlessly, refusing to let the betrayal go unanswered.

They weaved through narrow hallways, ducking and dodging, each manoeuvre calculated and executed precisely. Their footsteps echoed, intermingling with the sharp exhales of exertion.

As they emerged into a spacious courtyard, the chase spilt into the open air. The sun's rays beat down on them, casting long shadows on the ground, mirroring the darkness that had enveloped their relationship. Theo's voice reverberated, filled with frustration and anger.

Briggs's determination to retain possession of the file fueled his every move. He deflected Theo's attacks, skillfully avoiding his relentless pursuit.

Theo's resolve remained unyielding as he closed the gap between them, launching a final desperate lunge to regain control of the file. The air was tense as their hands collided, fingers grappling for possession. Their eyes locked, reflecting a mixture of determination, regret, and the shattered remnants of their friendship.

For a fleeting moment, time seemed to stand still. Their hands trembled, each man exerting his strength and willpower. The file hung precariously between them...

With a surge of adrenaline, Briggs managed to overpower Theo, his grip tightening around the file. He swiftly wrenched it from Theo's grasp, leaving him empty-handed and defeated.

Theo, breathless and defeated, watched as Briggs retreated, disappearing into the distance. A mix of emotions swirled within him—betrayal, anger, and a profound sense of loss.

In the aftermath of the chase, the reality of their choices sank in. Now in possession of the file, Briggs understood the gravity of his actions. The weight of guilt bore down upon him, mingling with the adrenaline that still coursed through his veins. He had to get out of there as soon as possible.

Quickly he got a cab that took him to the private agent aircraft that brought them to Cameroun. Briggs quickly boarded and ordered that the plane take off immediately before Theo could catch up.

A sense of relief washed over him as Briggs boarded the private agent aircraft. He believed he had successfully eluded Theo and his team, thinking he would finally have a moment of respite.

As the plane ascended into the sky, Briggs settled into his seat, unaware of the danger lurking in the cabin. The atmosphere inside the aircraft was tense, filled with a mix of anticipation and apprehension. The agents who had chosen to align themselves with Theo cast wary glances at Briggs, their loyalty now divided.

Suddenly, the cabin door swung open, revealing Theo with a wicked grin. He sauntered in, commanding attention and sending chills down Briggs' spine. The air grew heavy with tension as the other agents in the cabin shifted uncomfortably, unsure of what would unfold next.

Theo's eyes locked onto Briggs, a mixture of malice and triumph evident in his gaze. He slowly approached, his footsteps echoing through the confined space. Briggs felt a surge of adrenaline coursing through his veins, preparing himself for the inevitable confrontation.

Theo lunged at Briggs without speaking, engaging him in a fierce hand-to-hand combat. The plane shook and rattled as the two adversaries grappled with each other, their training and skills put to the test. The agents on board were torn between intervening or allowing the battle to unfold, unsure which side to support.

The struggle continued for an eternity, each punch and kick echoing through the cabin. The sound of scuffling feet and grunts of exertion filled the air. Sparks flew as their clashing wills ignited a fiery showdown.

Fueled by determination and desperation, Briggs managed to gain the upper hand momentarily. With a swift and calculated move, he disarmed Theo, clattering his gun to the floor. But before Briggs could secure his victory, the remaining agents who had sided with Theo converged on him, outnumbering him significantly.

Cornered and outnumbered, Briggs knew he had to act swiftly. His mind raced, searching for a way to turn the tables. With a surge of resilience, he launched a series of evasive manoeuvres, dodging the attacks of his former comrades while swiftly incapacitating them one by one. It was a battle of wits, agility, and sheer determination.

Finally, only Theo remained standing. He watched with fury and admiration as Briggs fought through the chaos. There was a flicker of recognition in his eyes, a reminder of the bond they once shared. But the allure of power and betrayal had clouded Theo's judgement, severing the ties that had once bound them.

Briggs lunged at Theo with renewed vigour, refusing to succumb to defeat. Blow after blow was exchanged, their bodies contorted in a combat dance. The plane rattled, its turbulence mirroring the intensity of the struggle. It became a battle not only for the file but for their fractured past and the future of their loyalty.

Briggs unleashed a devastating strike in a final, decisive moment, sending Theo crashing to the floor. Briggs stood over his fallen adversary, gasping for breath, bloodied and bruised. His heart pounded in his chest, his body ached from the exertion, but a sense of relief washed over him.

Immediately chaos engulfed the aircraft, the once-controlled environment descended into anarchy. The agents onboard, torn between loyalty and self-preservation, turned against each other, fueled by the intensity of their conflicting motives. Bullets whizzed through the air, shattering windows and puncturing metal, further intensifying the atmosphere of fear and uncertainty.

As the agents inside the plane grappled with their divided loyalties, chaos erupted in every corner of the cabin. Bullets whizzed through the air, creating a deadly symphony of gunfire. The once orderly space now resembled a battlefield, with agents turning against one another desperately struggling for control.

Amidst the mayhem, the deafening sound of an explosion reverberated through the plane. Panic surged as the aircraft shook violently, its structural integrity compromised. The bullet that had found its mark on one of the pilots had sent the plane into an uncontrolled descent, hurtling towards the earth below.

The atmosphere inside the cabin grew suffocating as smoke and the stench of burning metal filled the air. The plane's wings caught fire, casting an eerie glow across the chaotic scene. Fear etched itself onto the faces of the agents as they realized the dire situation they were in.

The spiralling descent of the aircraft only amplified the chaos already present. The force of the wind from the downward spiral whipped through the cabin, disorienting those still engaged in the frenzied conflict. The once-confined space became a maelstrom of flying objects, papers, and debris.

Struggling to maintain balance amidst the turbulence, Briggs fought against the odds to regain control. He knew that to survive, they needed to find a way to stabilize the plane and bring it to a controlled landing. As the chaos intensified, he mustered his remaining strength and focused on the task.

Clinging onto anything stable, Briggs managed to reach the cockpit. The plane shook violently, each jolt threatening to throw him off course. His determination fueled him, as he fought against the howling winds and swirling debris. With every step, he felt the weight of the situation pressing upon him.

Upon reaching the cockpit, Briggs surveyed the pilot's damage and lifeless body. Time was of the essence as he assessed the controls, attempting to regain control of the spiralling aircraft. His hands trembled with adrenaline as he tried to steady the plane's descent.

However, one of the agents launched at him, choking him with his arm and dragging him back to the passenger's seat.

That moment passengers and agents were thrown about, clinging desperately to anything within reach. The once-sturdy aircraft trembled under the strain, its structure threatening to give way at any moment. Flames erupted from the damaged wings, casting an eerie glow that danced through the cabin, painting the scene with a sinister hue.

Fear and panic gripped the hearts of those onboard as the realization of their impending doom set in. The desperate struggle for survival escalated to unimaginable levels. Agents, once colleagues and comrades, now fought ruthlessly, driven by the instinct to live another day.

Amidst the swirling madness, Briggs found himself caught in the crossfire. Dodging bullets and debris, he sought an escape, his survival instincts kicking into overdrive. His mind raced, analyzing the dire situation and searching for a way to turn the tides of fate in his favour.

Through the billowing smoke and the cacophony of screams, Briggs caught sight of an emergency exit. Determined, he fought his way towards it, relentlessly pushing through the throngs of desperate agents. Each step felt like an eternity, his heart pounding in his chest, the weight of the situation bearing down upon him.

As he neared the exit, a powerful gust of wind from the spiralling plane's descent rushed through the cabin. It amplified the chaos, whipping loose objects and bodies around like ragdolls. The unyielding force threatened to pull Briggs back into the chaos, but he clung to his resolve, refusing to be swept away.

Amidst the pandemonium, a figure emerged from the shadows. Theo, a trusted ally and friend, had seemingly swayed half of the agents to his side. Theo's sinister intentions were now laid bare, his gun pointed directly at Briggs, his gaze filled with a chilling mix of malice and triumph. The arm in which he used his gun was laced with his golden wristwatch.

A sudden interruption shattered the tension-filled air as Theo prepared to pull the trigger. Agent Sasha, who had remained true to the cause, emerged from the chaos, her determination cutting through the maelstrom of violence. With a swift and decisive shot, her bullet found its mark, striking Theo's chest with precision.

Time seemed to slow as Theo's body convulsed and was propelled towards the shattered window. His figure grew smaller and smaller, disappearing into the abyss of the sky, leaving only a faint echo of his malevolence behind. It was as if the chaos had swallowed him whole, erasing his existence from that fractured reality.

CHAPTER TEN

Briggs, dressed in a sleek dark suit and a fedora hat, stepped into the dimly lit warehouse. The air hung heavy with anticipation as he moved with calculated steps, his senses heightened, aware that he was not alone in the vast expanse of the space. His every move exuded an aura of purpose and determination.

He cast his gaze straight ahead, refusing to be distracted by the shadows that danced around him. His focus remained singular, fixated on his mission to confront Theo. Briggs knew that this encounter would be the defining moment, the culmination of their shared history of loyalty and betrayal.

As he stood in the stillness of the empty warehouse, a sense of quiet confidence emanated from him. He was prepared for whatever lay ahead, mentally and physically honed for the imminent confrontation. The silence stretched, broken only by the faint sounds of his own steady breaths.

Time seemed to stretch as Briggs stood patiently, waiting for Theo to reveal himself. The tension in the air thickened, anticipation mounting with each passing moment. The echoes of their past reverberated within him, memories intertwining with the present, fueling his resolve.

Suddenly, a sound disrupted the stillness. The soft click of a door latch echoed through the warehouse, alerting Briggs to the presence of an intruder. He remained rooted to the spot, his eyes trained on the source of the noise, ready to face Theo head-on.

A figure emerged from the shadows, slowly revealing itself. Theo stepped forward, his features etched with determination and defiance. There was a calculated calmness in his demeanour.

Theo and Briggs locked eyes, two formidable adversaries standing in the vast expanse of the warehouse. The weight of their shared past hung heavy in the air, the unspoken words echoing silently between them. At that moment, time seemed to stand still.

A silence enveloped the space, an unspoken agreement that this encounter would determine the course of their intertwined destinies. Their eyes mirrored the complex web of emotions — anger and betrayal.

Briggs broke the silence, his voice steady but tinged with an undercurrent of intensity. "Theo," he spoke, his words cutting through the air. "It ends here."

Theo's expression hardened, his gaze unwavering. He responded with a measured tone, each word laced with an underlying determination. "I'm afraid, old friend, it's only beginning."

With those words, the tension in the warehouse escalated. The anticipation crackled like electricity, their confrontation imminent. The space around them seemed to shrink, focusing solely on the clash of wills about to unfold.

Briggs and Theo assumed their stances, their bodies poised for action. The air became charged with anticipation, as if holding its breath in anticipation of the clash that would determine their fates.

In that moment, the echoes of their shared past, battles fought, and forged bonds reverberated through the warehouse. The once-unbreakable connection now severed by mistrust and diverging paths, forcing them into this final confrontation.

Briggs and Theo circled each other, their movements fluid yet deliberate. Their eyes remained locked, each attempting to decipher the other's intentions.

'Where's the wristwatch, Briggs? I know you still had it on you when the original file got lost in the crash.' his voice was filled with anger and frustration, Briggs's chuckle grew louder. He unhooked a wristwatch from his own hand and slid it across the floor towards Theo. With a mix of curiosity and growing anger, Theo picked up the watch, only to realise it wasn't Briggs's wristwatch's own, but his own; the one he had given to Durango, intending for it to reach Briggs.

The realisation hit Theo like a thunderbolt, his expression transforming from anger to a mix of fury and betrayal. His eyes locked with Briggs', a menacing glare on his face. "Where is it?!" he bellowed, his voice reverberating through the warehouse.

Briggs maintained his composure, his gaze unwavering. A wry smile played at the corners of his lips, a silent acknowledgement of his cunning. "Oh, Theo," he said, his voice dripping with amusement. "You underestimated me, my friend."

Theo's anger intensified, his fists clenched in frustration. The weight of his miscalculation bore down upon him, realising that Briggs had outmanoeuvred him at every turn. He felt a seething rage building within, threatening to consume him.

Theo's patience wore thin, his frustration boiling over. "Cut the games, Briggs! Where is the file? What have you done with it?" His voice trembled with anger and fear of losing control over the information that could change everything.

Briggs smirked, 'Come get it. Theo'

In a swift motion, Theo lunged at Briggs, their bodies colliding in a clash of strength and fury. The air crackled with energy as they grappled, their struggle mirroring the battle of ideals and loyalties within them.

Blows were exchanged, each strike fueling their thirst for retribution. The warehouse seemed to shrink around them, their fight a microcosm of the wider conflict that had consumed their lives. Metal crates rattled, their contents scattering in the wake of their relentless struggle.

As they fought, the backdrop of their fractured past unfolded before them. The memories of trust and camaraderie clashed with the painful reality of betrayal and manipulation. In their relentless pursuit of power and control, they had become mere pawns in a larger game.

Amidst the chaos of their physical confrontation, Theo's mind raced, searching for a way to gain the upper hand. He knew he couldn't let Briggs escape, couldn't allow him to continue his

As the fierce confrontation between Theo and Briggs raged on, it seemed that Theo had gained the upper hand. He sent Briggs crashing to the floor with a powerful blow, the impact reverberating through his body. The moment's weight pressed upon him, but Briggs refused to surrender.

Slowly, Briggs rose to his feet, his body aching from the impact. He took a deep breath, his eyes fixed on Theo, his resolve unyielding. The taste of his own blood lingered on his lips, a reminder of the stakes at hand.

In the face of adversity, Briggs tapped into a hidden reservoir of physical and mental strength. His mind focused, sharp, and calculated, as he regained his footing, determined not to be defeated. He knew he had to find a way to turn the tide, to regain control of the situation.

Theo watched, a mix of surprise and concern flickering across his face. He had underestimated Briggs, failing to consider the depths of his resilience. As Briggs steadied himself, a fire ignited, fueling his determination.

Briggs closed the distance between himself and Theo with each step, his movements deliberate and measured. His eyes locked onto Theo's, an unspoken challenge passing between them. There was no room for doubt or hesitation, only the unwavering focus on his objective.

As Briggs neared, the atmosphere in the warehouse shifted, charged with an undeniable tension. Time seemed to slow, each heartbeat echoing in his ears. He could hear the distant sounds of chaos around them, but his attention remained solely on Theo.

Theo braced himself, and prepared for Briggs' counterattack. But he hadn't anticipated the sheer determination emanating from his adversary. Briggs launched forward, channelling his strength and agility into a devastating countermove.

In a display of sheer force, Briggs unleashed a series of precise strikes, each blow aimed with purpose and precision.

Yet, Theo, driven by a potent mix of anger and betrayal, seemed to have gained the upper hand in their confrontation. With a forceful blow, he sent Briggs crashing to the ground, the impact reverberating through his body. The weight of his adversary pressed down on him, threatening to overwhelm his senses.

As Briggs lay sprawled on the floor, he took a moment to steady himself, his breath coming in ragged gasps. Pain coursed through his body, but he refused to succumb to defeat. With each passing second, he regained control, summoning his inner strength to rise once more.

Slowly, Briggs pushed himself off the ground, his muscles protesting with each movement. He steadied his breathing, his eyes never leaving Theo, who stood before him with a mixture of triumph and fury across his face.

Theo, momentarily intoxicated by his apparent victory, failed to anticipate the resilience burning within Briggs. Ignoring the pain coursing through his veins, Briggs focused his gaze on Theo, his eyes radiating a quiet determination.

As Briggs and Theo faced each other, their gazes locked in a tense standoff, a sudden disturbance shattered the fragile equilibrium of the warehouse. Durango, accompanied by a legion of his well-armed men, stormed into the facility with malicious intent. Their presence was a chilling reminder that the danger lurking in the shadows was far from over.

The room fell into a pregnant silence as Durango's men surrounded Briggs, their weapons poised and ready. The tension in the air thickened, Theo momentarily forgotten as a new threat emerged. Briggs stood defiantly, his eyes flickering with apprehension and determination.

But just as all hope seemed lost, a seismic shift occurred. The sound of heavy footsteps reverberated through the warehouse, drawing the attention of both parties. Alexander Q's men, donned in sleek armour and brandishing an impressive array of weaponry, stormed into the facility like an unstoppable force.

A collective gasp echoed as Durango's men focused on this unexpected intrusion. The balance of power teetered precariously, the room a powder keg waiting to explode. The eyes of Alexander Q's men met those of Briggs, waiting for his command, ready to follow his lead.

Steady and resolute, Briggs sensed the moment's weight upon his shoulders. The tides had turned, and he knew he had a choice to make—one that would shape the outcome of this battle. His mind raced, weighing the risks and considering the consequences.

Briggs issued his command in a voice that carried the weight of authority. "Stand down," he ordered, his tone firm and unwavering. The words hung in the air, declaring his determination to end this cycle of violence.

Durango's men hesitated, their eyes darting between their leader and the newly arrived force. The uncertain silence stretched as if time held its breath, waiting for the resolution of this clash of wills.

With a calculating gleam in his eyes, Durango realised the tides had turned against him. He reluctantly nodded to his men.

Briggs turned to face Theo, his eyes burning with determination and anger. He took a deep breath, steadying himself before he spoke.

'I have the file, Theo. I have the wristwatch. But let me clarify—I'll never let someone as evil as you get your hands on them.' Briggs said

Theo's expression hardened, a flicker of annoyance crossing his face.

'You're a fool, Briggs. You think you can stop me? I've always been one step ahead of you.'

Briggs's voice was laced with resolve as he looked straight into Theo's eyes.

'Maybe you have been, Theo. But not this time. You've crossed a line. You almost killed a friend of mine—Christopher. You don't get to walk away from that unscathed.'

Theo's face betrayed a hint of surprise as if he hadn't expected Briggs to mention Christopher's name. He chuckled slightly.

'Christopher? The little man. He's the one you're worried about?'

Briggs's anger flared, his voice filled with righteous fury.

Theo's eyes narrowed, his face contorted with anger and defiance.

'You think you can defeat me, Briggs? You're underestimating my power and influence.'

Briggs's voice grew colder, his words dripping with determination.

'It's not just about defeating you, Theo. It's about bringing justice to those you've hurt, about making sure that evil like you doesn't go unpunished. I won't rest until you pay for your crimes.'

Theo's facade of confidence wavered for a moment, replaced by a flicker of uncertainty. He clenched his fists, seemingly grappling with his next move.

'You'll regret this, Briggs. I promise you that.'

Briggs's gaze remained unwavering, his resolve unshakeable.

'No, Theo. It's you who will regret the choices you've made. The consequences are catching up to you, and I'm here to ensure they do.'

Briggs turned to Q's men. 'Now!' he yelled

As the command left Briggs's lips, his voice echoed with authority, igniting a surge of determination in the hearts of Alexander Q's men. They charged forward with a resolute battle cry, their footsteps thundering against the cold concrete floor.

Durango's men, caught off guard by the sudden assault, scrambled to defend themselves. But the sheer force and ferocity of Alexander Q's elite team were overwhelming. Bullets whizzed through the air, finding their targets with deadly precision. The warehouse erupted into chaos as the clash of metal and the crackle of gunfire filled the space.

At the forefront of the charge, Briggs pursued Theo and Durango with unwavering resolve. The weight of his past experiences, sacrifices, and loyalty to his fallen comrade, Christopher, fueled his every step. He was fueled by a relentless thirst for justice and a desire to ensure that no one else would suffer at the hands of Theo's treachery.

Theo and Durango, realising they were outnumbered and outmatched, fought back desperately. They fired rounds into the sea of oncoming agents, creating temporary barriers with crates and machinery to slow down their pursuers. But it was only a matter of time before the combined force of Briggs and Alexander Q's men closed in on them.

As they neared their targets, a renewed surge of adrenaline coursed through Briggs's veins. He leapt over obstacles and dodged bullets, his every movement calculated and precise. With unwavering focus, he closed the distance between himself and Theo, his eyes locked on his former friend turned enemy.

Meanwhile, Alexander Q's men relentlessly pursued, ensuring that Durango and his remaining followers were pushed back, their options dwindling with each passing second. The once-thriving chaos transformed into a scene of controlled aggression as the tide turned decisively against the perpetrators of darkness.

Briggs finally cornered Theo, who was isolated and devoid of escape routes. The air crackled with tension as the two adversaries faced each other, their eyes locked in a fierce battle of wills. The warehouse's dim lighting cast long shadows, heightening the dramatic atmosphere.

Without a word, Briggs lunged forward, his movements fluid and precise. Theo, caught off guard by the sudden assault, barely managed to defend himself. Blow after blow rained down, each strike fueled by anger, vengeance, and a desire to end Theo's reign of terror.

In the periphery of his vision, Briggs could see the remnants of Durango's forces being overwhelmed by the relentless assault of Alexander Q's men. The tide had turned definitively, and justice was finally being served.

As Theo's resistance weakened, his defiance wavered, giving way to a mix of fear and defeat. Briggs's fists continued to pummel him, the physicality mirroring the emotional turmoil that had plagued their relationship since their paths diverged.

With one final strike, Briggs brought Theo to his knees. The room fell silent, except for the ragged breaths and the distant commotion of the ongoing battle. Briggs stood over his fallen foe, his chest heaving with exhaustion but his eyes ablaze with triumph.

Theo defeated and broken, looked up at Briggs, a mixture of bitterness and resignation etched across his face. Both men knew their journey had reached its bitter end at that moment. The legacy of their friendship shared history, and choices culminated in this final confrontation.

However, as Briggs turned around to leave, Theo quickly rushed to his feet, pushed him off and ran out of the space. Briggs recovering from this, followed him, trying to catch up with Theo. But to his surprise, there was an awaiting helicopter outside for Theo.

As Briggs closed in on Theo, his adversary's desperation peaked. With a sudden burst of agility, Theo skillfully evaded Briggs's final blow and darted towards the awaiting helicopter. Whirring blades filled the air as the helicopter's engine roared to life.

Briggs watched in frustration as Theo leapt into the helicopter, his escape seemingly imminent. Determined not to let him slip away, Briggs quickly surveyed his surroundings for a solution. His eyes landed on a nearby stack of crates, and without hesitation, he dashed towards them.

With sheer determination, Briggs manoeuvred through the maze of obstacles, expertly navigating the chaotic scene. The intensity of the pursuit heightened as he closed the distance between himself and the fleeing helicopter. Time seemed to slow down as Briggs prepared himself for a final, daring move.

But it was too late. He couldn't catch up with Theo as Theo's helicopter lifted off into the sky. Briggs stood on the ground, watching its departure with a mix of frustration and determination. Theo watched him from the other end of the plane. The exchange of glances between them held an unspoken understanding that their paths would cross again.

With the dust settling and the chaos subsiding, Briggs took a moment to gather his thoughts. The warehouse, now empty and devoid of the frenetic energy that had consumed it moments before, was a stark reminder of the challenges ahead. The mission to bring down Theo and dismantle the nefarious network he had become a part of was far from complete.

As Briggs surveyed the scene, he noticed the remaining members of Durango's defeated forces regrouping, their expressions a mix of confusion and surrender. The tide had turned against them, and their loyalty to Durango wavered in the face of such overwhelming opposition.

Briggs, fueled by the adrenaline coursing through his veins, knew this was a critical moment. He needed to gather any information he could from the defeated members of Durango's organization before they had a chance to regroup or retreat. Taking command of the situation, he directed his fellow agents to secure and interrogate the captured individuals.

While going through with the captives, he noted a familiar figure trying to escape through the shadows and went after him. Durango made his way out of the facility as first as he could.

Briggs swiftly moved in, his heart pounding with adrenaline as he closed in on Durango. He had come too far to let him escape. With a determined grip on his gun, Briggs aimed carefully, his eyes locked on Durango's fleeing figure. Time seemed to slow down as he squeezed the trigger, and three shots echoed through the air.

The first bullet grazed Durango's shoulder, causing him to stumble, but he managed to regain his balance and kept running. Briggs knew he had to stop him before he disappeared into the shadows. With unwavering focus, he fired the second shot, aiming for Durango's leg. The bullet found its mark, causing Durango to cry out in pain as he fell to the ground. His momentum abruptly halted.

As Durango hit the floor, Briggs closed the distance between them, his heart pounding with anger, frustration, and a lingering sense of justice. Durango struggled to rise, his eyes filled with desperation and fear, realizing his attempts to escape had been thwarted.

Briggs stood over him, his gaze piercing and resolute. "It ends here, Durango," he declared, his voice firm and unwavering. "You've caused enough pain and destruction. It's time to face the consequences of your actions."

Durango gasped for breath, his eyes flickering with defiance and resignation. He knew his time was up, and there was no escape from the reckoning that awaited him. Slowly, he raised his hands in surrender, acknowledging the futility of resistance.

Briggs wasted no time. With a swift motion, he holstered his weapon and swiftly restrained Durango, securing his hands with handcuffs. He ensured they were tight, ensuring Durango wouldn't attempt any further acts of defiance.

As he stood there, victorious yet weary, Briggs couldn't help but think of Christopher, his dear friend who had been a victim of Durango's cruelty. The memory of Christopher's wounded body in the hospital bed fueled his determination to bring Durango to justice.

With Durango apprehended, Briggs reached for his communication device and alerted his team of the successful capture. Reinforcements arrived shortly after, securing the area and ensuring Durango's transportation to a secure facility.

As the commotion settled, Briggs took a moment to catch his breath. He felt a mix of emotions wash over him—relief, satisfaction, and a sense of emptiness. The mission had taken its toll, and he couldn't help but wonder what lay ahead in his pursuit of justice.

But for now, Briggs stood tall, knowing that he had accomplished what he had set out to do. Durango was in custody, and the threat he posed had been neutralised. As he looked back at the warehouse, his eyes focused on the distant horizon, filled with determination. The battle may not be over, but he was ready to face whatever challenges lay ahead, knowing that justice would prevail.

Briggs entered Alexander Q's office the next day, accompanied by a group of senior agents. The atmosphere in the room was tense, as everyone present knew the gravity of the situation and the implications it held for their organisation. They had all gathered to hear Briggs's detailed report of the events that unfolded and the revelation of Theo's involvement in the terrorist network.

As Briggs stood before the high-ranking officers, he could feel their piercing gaze fixed upon him.

Alexander Q, a seasoned agent with a commanding presence, sat behind his desk, his expression inscrutable. The room was filled with expectation, and the weight of their collective responsibility hung heavily in the air.

Briggs took a deep breath, steeling himself for the task at hand. His voice was steady as he began recounting the previous day's events. He spoke with clarity and precision, carefully detailing how the terrorist network had emerged from within their own ranks, catching them off guard.

As he revealed Theo's involvement, a hushed silence filled the room. The tension escalated as the officers exchanged glances and absorbed the gravity of the situation. The betrayal of one of their own was a bitter pill, and the consequences reverberated through their ranks.

Q's brooding look intensified, his eyes narrowing as he listened intently to Briggs's account. It was clear that he was deeply troubled by the revelations. The room seemed to shrink under the weight of their collective unease as they grappled with the implications of Theo's actions and the need to address the internal security breach.

Briggs continued, describing the intense pursuit and confrontation with Theo and Durango. He didn't deny that Durango had met his end during the altercation. The news of his arrest hung heavy in the room.

As Briggs concluded his report, the room fell into a profound silence. The officers exchanged glances, their expressions a mix of concern, anger, and determination. The truth had been laid bare, and it was clear that there were significant challenges ahead. The organisation would need to reckon with its vulnerabilities, address the internal flaws, and ensure that such a breach of trust would never happen again.

Q finally spoke, his voice measured but tinged with a steely resolve. "Thank you, Briggs," he said, his gaze piercing. "Your dedication and bravery have not gone unnoticed. We find ourselves facing an internal threat of unprecedented magnitude. We must act swiftly and decisively to root out any remaining elements of this network and restore trust within our ranks."

The tension in the room remained palpable, but there was also a shared sense of determination. The past few days' events had shaken them to the core, but they were united in their resolve to rebuild and strengthen their organization. They all understood the weight of their responsibility and the importance of regaining control.

Q's words echoed in their minds as they dispersed from the office. The road ahead would be arduous, requiring diligent investigation, comprehensive security measures, and a renewed commitment to their mission. They must work shoulder to shoulder-together to rebuild their organization's integrity and prevent future breaches.

As the silence lingered, Briggs mustered the courage to voice his decision. "Gentlemen," he began, his voice steady but tinged with a hint of vulnerability, "I have come to a realization during these recent events. My dedication to this agency has been unwavering, but I must prioritize my family above all else. With a heavy heart, I inform you of my decision to retire."

The room fell silent once again, the weight of Briggs's words hanging in the air. The officers exchanged glances, understanding the significance of his choice. While some might have expected surprise or even resistance, they recognized the depth of his commitment and the validity of his reasoning.

As the weight of the situation settled upon Briggs, he came to a profound realization. Despite his dedication and achievements in the agency, he now understood the true importance of family. Recent events had underscored life's fragility and the need to cherish the moments with loved ones.

Briggs felt a deep longing for a different kind of fulfilment in that tense room as the officers absorbed the shocking revelations. Pursuing justice and protecting the world had been his calling for many years, but now he yearned for something more personal—a sense of belonging and the opportunity to create lasting memories with his family.

Alexander Q, broke the silence with a nod of understanding. "Briggs, your contributions to this agency are immeasurable, and we respect your decision," he said, his tone filled with appreciation and regret. "Your service has been exemplary, and your dedication has never wavered. It is only fitting that you now prioritize your family and embrace the next chapter of your life."

Alexander Q proceeded. He looked Briggs in the eye and asked, "Do you understand the consequences of your action? By retiring, you may become a target for the very shadows you once hunted. Are you prepared to face them alone?"

Briggs took a moment to consider Q's words. He understood the gravity of the situation, the potential risks he might face as a retired agent. But his resolve remained unshaken. With a steely determination, he met Q's gaze and replied, "I am fully aware of the consequences, Alexander. I have spent my entire career facing shadows and am ready to confront them should they dare to return. I will not cower in fear. I will be waiting."

Q nodded a mixture of admiration and concern visible in his eyes. "Briggs, your bravery and dedication have always been commendable," Q said, his voice laced with caution. "But I implore you to remain vigilant. The shadows can be relentless and may strike when you least expect it. If the time comes when you need assistance, do not hesitate to reach out. You may have retired from the agency but will remain part of our family forever."

Briggs replied with a heartfelt nod of gratitude, "Thank you, Alexander. Your words mean a great deal to me. Rest assured, I will not hesitate to seek aid if the shadows become overwhelming. But for now, I must prioritise my family and the life that awaits me outside the agency. I will carry the lessons and values I have learned and face whatever challenges come my way." Briggs saluted and left the room.

As Briggs left the room, he carried a sense of purpose, strengthened by the knowledge that he was not alone in his retirement. He knew his former colleagues would continue their tireless pursuit of justice, even as he embarked on a different path.

As he stepped into the next chapter of his life, Briggs embraced the newfound freedom and the opportunity to nurture and protect his family. He knew that the shadows might cast their menacing presence at some point, but he was prepared to face them head-on, fortified by his unwavering determination and the love surrounding him.

Briggs entered the hospital room where Christopher lay, still unconscious. Rachel stood by his side. They exchanged a concerned glance before Briggs approached her, his heart heavy with emotions.

'Rachel, how is he doing?' Briggs said softly.

Rachel rose gently so as not to disturb Christopher. 'He's recovering, Briggs. The doctors say he just needs more time. We need to be patient.' she replied, turning to Christopher to see if he was holding up well.

Briggs took a deep breath, feeling a mix of relief and worry flood through him. At that moment, he realised how much he cherished Rachel and how their bond had grown stronger amidst the chaos and danger they had faced together.

'Rachel? Turn around...' Briggs said.

Rachel turned her attention to Briggs, her eyes filled with curiosity and a hint of anticipation.

Briggs pulled out a small box. 'Rachel, you've been my rock throughout all these trials and challenges. You've stood by my side, offering unwavering support and love. I can't imagine my life without you.'

Rachel's eyes widened, surprise and joy spreading across her face. She could sense the gravity of what was about to happen.

Briggs opened the box to reveal a ring. 'Rachel, Marry me.'

Rachel gasped, her hand instinctively moving to cover her mouth in disbelief. Tears welled up in her eyes as she nodded, unable to find her voice. Overwhelmed with emotions, she finally managed to whisper a heartfelt "Yes."

Briggs smiled, a mix of happiness and relief washing over him. He gently slipped the ring onto Rachel's finger, sealing their commitment to one another. At that moment, the world around them seemed to fade away, leaving only the profound connection between them.

As Briggs and Rachel embraced, their hearts filled with gratitude and anticipation for the future that awaited them. They were ready to face whatever came their way, hand in hand, with unwavering love and an unbreakable bond. In that hospital room, amidst beeping monitors and the scent of antiseptic, their love story continued to unfold, promising a future filled with hope, resilience, and the enduring power of love.

THE END

Printed in Great Britain
by Amazon

24176299R00229